BENEATH THE MASK

MARG MCALISTER

Blue Gem Publishing

Also by Marg McAlister

GEORGIE B. GOODE BOOKS

SERIES 1

Good to Go

Georgie Be Good

Good Riddance

Up to No Good

In Good Hands

Too Good to be True

As Good as It Gets

Good Golly Miss Molly

Good Vibrations

A Rocking Good Christmas

SERIES 2

Good Intentions

A Good Result

No Good Reason

Good Fortune

This edition published by Blue Gem Publishing in 2022.

Title: Beneath The Mask | Marg McAlister, author

ISBN: 978-1-922772-29-9 (Paperback edition)

ISBN: 978-1-922772-69-5 (Ebook edition)

Cover Design by Annie Moril

V24032022

Valentine's Gifts

Tuesdays and Thursdays were 13-year-old Tammy Dyson's favorite days of the week for a very good reason.

Her brother Garrett wasn't home early enough to torture her.

On those two days, Garrett stayed back after school to train with the football team. A handsome boy of seventeen who also happened to be the star quarterback, he always had a couple of the cheerleaders hovering, hoping for a crumb of attention after training finished. Usually, he didn't get home until right on supper time or even later, which was okay with his proud mama and tolerated by his stern father. Garrett was the kind of son everyone wanted, so you had to cut him some slack.

It was fine with Tammy, too, because her psychopath-in-disguise brother couldn't go after her with that feral glint in his eye. On other days, he was fond of dogging her footsteps on the track down to the farm after they got off the school bus, using his laser-sharp intelligence to dissect her friends, her test results, her appearance. One little barb after another. Sometimes, her older brother Kyle would time his lift home from his uncle Rocky's farm to coincide with the school bus, and then the two of them would join forces to tease her.

That's what they called it. *Teasing.*

If something hadn't gone Garrett's way at school, he'd show his game face to everyone else—charming, polite, reasonable Garrett—and wait to take it out on Tammy. He'd push her around a little or herd her in front of him and back her up against a tree, forcing her chin up to look him in the eye while he said horrible things, used words that his mother and father had never heard him say.

As a child, Tammy had tried, many times, to summon up enough courage to tell her parents what was going on, despite Garrett's threats that she'd regret it if she told. She had learned as a preschooler that Garrett's version would always be believed before hers, but that didn't stop her from trying to seek justice as she grew older.

Garrett denied any wrongdoing every time. Garrett with his sky-blue, innocent eyes, his hurt expression, his air of bafflement—his face telegraphing, *why would my sister say things like this?*

Once, he made sure that his mother was listening when he said softly to eleven-year-old Tammy, "Why? All these lies, all the time." He heaved a baffled sigh. "What have I ever done to you?"

That day, even her beloved mother cast a slightly doubtful look at Tammy.

The second time, aware that his father was lurking

nearby, he had muttered, "One day, Tammy, you'll admit that I never did any of the things you accuse me of. But it'll be too late to apologize because a guy can only take so much." He'd moved away, despondency in every bone of his body, and the next moment she felt her father's iron-like grip on her arm as he shook her with barely restrained violence.

"You don't deserve a brother like Garrett, you conniving little… little *miss,*" he'd hissed at her. Her father never swore, but she could tell he was inches from it on that day. "You've been a liar all your life, and one day you'll get what you deserve." He shoved her away from him, and Tammy almost fell, stumbling against the kitchen table. She gasped from the grip of his hard hands and the pain in her hip from the impact, which made it a trio because the abrasion on her knee was still bleeding after Garrett had tripped her.

"We were racing to the house," was Garrett's aggrieved version. "Just a bit of fun. Tammy tripped over." Shaking his head at her, he added, "I even went back and helped her up. Honestly, Tammy…."

Garrett would always win.

But right now, on Tuesday, he was blitzing it on the football training field and no doubt lining up one of his covert late-night meetings with Britney Thomas, so Tammy was safe.

Her other brother, Kyle, was also absent on Tuesdays, staying late to help out his Uncle Rocky on a neighboring farm. Tammy had no idea what 'helping out' meant, since her uncle no longer did any actual farming as far as she could determine. Still, she didn't care as long as Kyle was somewhere else. He didn't have

Garrett's creativity when it came to hurting her. His taunts were blunter and his handling rougher, but she knew that for both siblings, she was a convenient whipping boy. Or rather, girl.

On Tuesdays, she was free from them for hours.

She knew why they disliked her so much. She was the apple of their mother Susannah's eye, the pretty and talented little girl that Susannah had always wanted. A daughter that she could dress up, play with, sing to and laugh with. Tammy and Susannah both had naturally sunny, loving personalities, and Susannah had adored Tammy from the moment she entered the world.

Her brothers had sniffed out a rival instantly, peering into the carry-basket when Susannah brought their sister home from the hospital. Susannah had laughed about it when she told Tammy the story of her arrival.

"I remember taking you into the house and showing you to your brothers for the first time," she said, smiling indulgently. "And oh, their little faces! They were so jealous!" She chuckled. "Young rascals. Kyle's face was as black as thunder: he ordered me to take you back. He looked just like your Uncle Rocky when he's in a temper." She gave a mock shudder. "But he was only five. Of course he thought you were a rival, poor little mite."

Tammy hadn't laughed. When she was having this conversation with her mother, Tammy had turned six, just a little older than Kyle had been when his baby sister came home. By then, she had suffered enough at his hands to know that he meant every word he had said, even at five.

"And Garrett. He was just four, then. Do you know the first thing he said?"

Tammy did know; she'd heard the story before, but she went along with it. "Yes. He said that I stole his birthday."

"I've already told you, I know." Susannah ruffled Tammy's hair. "It was so funny. Every birthday I would say, "You are my best Valentine's Day present ever!" I would give him chocolate and flowers. So you can imagine how he felt when you were born on his birthday. As though you'd stolen it away. Now I have to give two of my babies chocolate and flowers!"

"Three, actually," Tammy said. "You don't let Kyle miss out."

"That's right. I love you all." Susannah gathered her up and squeezed her tight. "But you are my very favorite baby girl."

Tammy smiled reluctantly. "You don't have any other girls."

"And I always, *always* wanted a girl. I'm going to teach you so much: to cook and sing and act, and we're going to be friends forever."

At that moment, over her mother's shoulder, Tammy had seen Garrett watching, his blue eyes as cold as ice, and felt something inside herself shrivel.

And as for her father…his reaction to her arrival had, she guessed, had been similar to Kyle's, although he hid it better. Over the years, it had become clear to Tammy that Danny Dyson regarded her as a rival for his wife's affection. He had managed to minimize Susannah's influence on his sons by imposing harsh discipline and warning his wife against spoiling them. He didn't want them turning them into Momma's boys, he told her sternly.

Reluctantly, she mainly had complied, guiltily

sneaking in cuddles and kisses when Danny wasn't looking.

But when her daughter arrived, she became unexpectedly stubborn.

"No, Danny," she would say in her sweet southern voice, smiling up at him with her huge blue eyes, so like Garrett's and Tammy's. "A little girl needs cuddles. Before we know it, she'll be at school and growing up too fast. Let me have this time with her." She accompanied her entreaty with a kiss and an embrace for her husband, and Danny reluctantly complied. His beautiful wife Susannah was his one weakness.

Through the years, Tammy had learned to be quiet and biddable when her father was around, just as she eventually learned to bite her lip and say nothing when her brothers hurt her with words or deeds. When she entered her teens, she consoled herself with the thought that they would soon be adults and leave home, and it would be just herself and her Mom.

And her father, of course, but she had learned to steer clear of Danny Dyson.

Then her mother got sick.

First, it seemed like a general malaise, which Susannah waved off. Then some pain, and nausea, and several visits to the doctor. Then, a week ago, her mother had been whisked off to the hospital for tests.

Tammy, worried about her mother, had a terrible feeling that her life was going to get much, much worse —and on a day when she should have been able to relax because she had a few hours free from her brothers, Tammy was more scared than she'd ever been in her whole life.

Because today was the day her father was bringing Mom home from the hospital, and from a few terse comments made over the past few days, Tammy knew she was still sick.

Very sick.

Coming Home

TAMMY PROWLED RESTLESSLY around the house for nearly an hour before she finally heard the sound of her father's pickup coming along the lane from the main road. She ran to the door and down the front steps and stopped short, warned by the set expression on her father's face.

When he wore that expression, he was at his cold, hard worst.

Her eyes flicked to her mother sitting beside him, her face a pale blur through the windscreen. It was all Tammy could do not to run to her.

The driver's door opened, and her father got out. For a moment, his eyes rested on Tammy, and she almost rocked back at the anger and bitterness she saw there.

Pure rejection.

Inside, she felt an inch high, but she took a trembling step forward anyway. "Mom?"

Her father held up a hand, stopped her. "Stay there. Your mother's ill; don't bother her now." His voice was like a whip, but when he walked around to the passenger side and opened the door, his tone immediately became gentle. "Susannah, sweetheart? Let me help you inside."

Tammy clenched her teeth so hard that pain shot through her jaw. She watched, numb, holding on to the rail by the steps, while her father escorted her mother inside, one slow step at a time.

Her mother managed a smile that held traces of her usual sweetness, but Tammy could see the struggle as she inched up the steps. "Tammy, love. I'm all right. Just a little tired." She reached out and touched her arm. "A nice cup of coffee, perhaps?"

Tammy nodded, walking in slowly behind her parents, but once inside, her father shot another grim look her way. He kept his voice tender for his wife. "I don't know that coffee would be a good idea, Susannah. You're on painkillers, and you need lots of rest."

"Of course, you're right. Maybe Tammy can just come and sit with me, then."

"I will, Mom," Tammy said quickly.

"I'll sit with you, sweetness and light," her father said. "Tammy, make yourself useful and put supper on." He steered his wife into the bedroom.

Tammy stood, irresolute, not quite brave enough to go into the bedroom anyway. She desperately needed to hold her mother's hand and talk to her.

What could he do, anyway? Make her bend over the fence outside and whup her? He'd tried that only once in his life, and Tammy's mother, Danny Dyson's biddable, loving wife Susannah, hadn't spoken to him for two days. Never again, she'd made him promise.

But her mother was bedridden, and Danny Dyson

knew that Tammy wouldn't say a word for fear of worrying her Mom.

The bedroom door slammed in her face, and Tammy went to string some beans and peel potatoes.

Her father didn't come out until her brothers were home. She heard a truck lumbering up the drive and the sound of Kyle's voice yelling goodbye to his Uncle Rocky. He walked inside, saw her at the stovetop, and made a face. "You cooking again? Think I just lost my appetite."

She ignored that. Kyle would eat anything.

"Mom's home," she said, turning off the gas flame under the beans and carrots.

Something in her voice made Kyle abandon his usual efforts to bully her. "She all right?"

"She says she's okay. That she's just tired." She checked the potatoes before glancing at him. "But she looks sick. Dad's in with her."

"Huh." He disappeared, and she heard him tapping on her parents' bedroom door, then the murmur of voices.

That would be right. Kyle was allowed to see his mother, but not Tammy.

Kyle came out, went into the sitting room, and switched on the TV.

Fifteen minutes later, Garrett swaggered through the door, glowing with the after-effects of a hard workout followed by a shower and female adulation. Clearly, football training had gone well.

He saw her sitting at the table, staring into space

amid the place settings waiting for supper, and glanced at the pots on the stove. He groaned and walked past her to inspect the contents of the saucepans and the oven, then clipped her on the back of the head on the way back. "Cottage pie and veg again?"

Then why don't you learn to cook? She thought but bit her lip and said nothing.

He walked out, and she heard him talking to Kyle before he went to see their mother. This time, she heard Susannah's soft tones and a tired laugh.

Happy to see her golden boy, her best Valentine's Day present ever: Garrett.

Tammy choked back tears and shoved back her chair. She was going to see her mother, whatever the consequences.

She passed Garrett in the hall, and out of habit, he crowded her, grinning as he pushed her against the wall. With her heart in her mouth, Tammy opened the door.

Her father scowled. "I told you, your mother needs rest."

Keeping her voice mild and reasonable, Tammy forced a smile. "I just wanted to let you know that supper is ready." She walked to the other side of the bed and took her mother's hand, stroking it gently. "I'm glad you're home, Mom. I'm sorry you're sick."

Her mother's eyes filled. "Oh darling, I'm fine. It's so good to see you again. I missed you while I was in the hospital."

"I wanted to come and see you," Tammy said bravely—or stupidly, she wasn't sure—"but Dad thought it was best to let you have as much rest as possible." She didn't look at her father, knowing she'd pay for her insubordination later.

"Just seeing you would have made me feel better." Susannah sent a quick, reproachful look at her husband. "Tammy would never tire me, Danny."

"Would you like some supper?" asked Tammy. "I can bring you a tray."

Her mother smiled at her, but weariness lined her face. "You're kind, darling, but I'm really not hungry. Thank you for looking after the boys for me while I was away."

"I was happy to," Tammy lied. "Can I sit with you for a while after supper?"

Her father's voice, tight with annoyance, broke in. "You need to do your homework."

"I've done it." Tammy finally raised her eyes and looked at him, and the coldness in his eyes made her quail. "While I was waiting for you and Mom."

"Let her sit with me, Danny. I need to have my little girl with me for a while."

Unable to resist the note of pleading in his wife's voice, Danny gave a short, sharp nod. "All right. After supper, just for half an hour. Then you sleep."

"Thank you, darling." Her mother's eyes drifted closed, and her father jerked his head toward the door.

Silently, Tammy released her mother's hand and retreated.

It was time for supper with three males who barely tolerated her.

She swallowed hard and made her way to the kitchen.

Rules

Danny Dyson smoothed his wife's soft blonde hair and brushed his knuckles across her cheek. Her lips curved in a semblance of a smile, but she didn't open her eyes. "Danny," she murmured softly, and then drifted away, the meds kicking in.

All too soon, she would never open those beautiful blue eyes again.

Danny felt like raising his head and howling, like a wolf in pain. Susannah, the one thing in his life he had ever really cared about, would be gone from his life. He wanted to hit out, smash things, make someone suffer for it.

Two months, they'd said, maybe three. Palliative care was available, counselors, home help... and already, Marie from the church had offered to organize a roster of women to cook and clean and sit with Susannah while she went through radiotherapy or chemo or whatever was necessary.

None of it, he knew now, would help. The secondary tumors were everywhere, and he wasn't going to put Susannah through anything that wasn't going to see her life extended by years. They had both agreed that quality of life was important.

She would stay in her own home with her husband and children. All he could do was wait and watch her waste away.

His mind turned to his children, out there waiting for him to join them. He'd have to tell them. Between the three of them, he thought savagely; they'd be able to cope for all but a few hours in the middle of the day. He didn't want strangers in the house, not even from the church, intruding on the last of his time with Susannah.

Tammy could cook the evening meals; she had plenty of time after school. She could care for her mother while he got on with earning a living; he couldn't afford to let things slide now. He had too many balls in the air.

The thought of his daughter twisted his gut; Susannah always had, in his opinion, spent too much time pandering to young Tammy, filling her head with romantic nonsense from those old movies they loved to watch together and unrealistic ideas about being a singer or an actress.

The girl needed to realize that life was about more than romance and dancing in the rain. Her mother had found fulfillment in singing with the church choir; Tammy could do the same.

Tammy would end up managing the house, he supposed. In a couple more years, she could legally leave school and look after him and the boys. Until then, they'd cope.

The boys. He exhaled, nodding to himself. Both boys had potential. Kyle didn't have book smarts, but he could be a tradesman, work with Rocky. Knowing exactly how Kyle was helping out Rocky now, his father could picture plenty of benefits from that in years to come. Garrett, though—he was the one who had real potential. A son to make a man proud.

Go to college, get football out of his system, and then he'd be back home. Then, his father could take him fully into his confidence and start his real education.

Danny Dyson knew how to make money while the sheep went on their unsuspecting way. He had plenty of respect in the community while he worked behind the scenes, quietly amassing wealth.

Life would have been perfect if only fate hadn't stepped in to take Susannah early.

He stood for a moment and breathed deeply, waiting out the wave of grief, and then went out to do what had to be done.

His children were waiting, and Danny Dyson had never been one to avoid an unpleasant duty.

All three faces turned to him. Tammy's big blue eyes, so like Susannah's, were filled with apprehension, but she stood up and silently started ladling vegetables onto plates. He stared at the offering. Potatoes, beans, carrots. They looked limp. Then the cottage pie, which by now had dried out.

Danny looked at the meal and sighed. The girl would have to do better than this.

"I'm sorry," she said, almost inaudibly. "I had to keep it warm for too long."

"No excuses," he said. "A meal's edible, or it's not.

But now you have no choice: you'll have to learn."

He had deliberately made the last sentence ominous, and he could see his words hit home.

Her lower lip trembled. "What did the doctor say?"

"First, we eat. Then we talk." He put up a hand when she opened her mouth again in protest. "Garrett, say grace, if you please."

Garrett complied, looking suitably solemn, and they all ate in silence. Tammy, head down, managed a few mouthfuls and then just pushed the food around on her plate, but a few sharp words had her forcing it down. Nobody at Danny Dyson's table wasted food.

He waited until Tammy cleared the table, and all three were sitting, looking at him.

He made it quick and clean.

"Your mother has terminal cancer," he said, keeping his pace measured. "There is no cure, and there will be no remission. She has two, maybe three months."

Tammy sat frozen, staring at him. Garrett and Kyle exchanged glances, and then Garrett sat up straighter, his blue eyes resolute as he looked steadily at his father. His voice shook a little, but he stayed strong. "I'm so sorry, Dad. We'll do what we can to help you and make her last days comfortable."

The pride in his youngest son almost choked him. "Thank you, Garrett. I know you'll step up."

Kyle chimed in, parroting his brother. "Yeah, we'll help. Uh, do stuff. Whatever you want."

They all looked at Tammy. She closed her eyes and dropped her head onto her hands, and emitted a low, agonized moan, her shoulders shaking.

"We're all hurting," Danny said sharply, disgusted with her. "Your brothers have set you an example,

Tammy. Grow a backbone and do what needs to be done. Crying won't help your mother."

She shook her head, not looking at him, tears spilling through her fingers.

His voice grew harsher. "The women from the church mean well, but I don't want the house full of strangers from dawn till dusk. Tammy, look at me."

She kept her head bowed, and he had to make an effort to stay seated, not get up and jerk her up out of her seat, send her to her room.

"*Look at me.* And stop your crying." He made his voice measured. "Or you can forget about going in to sit with your mother."

That did the trick. Tammy wiped her eyes on her sleeve and sat up, mutinously meeting his eyes.

Danny drew in a deep breath. Much as he loved Susannah, she had ruined this child, making her soft and too free with her opinions. The girl thought she could get away with insubordination and lies about her brothers, escaping her needed discipline.

That would all change now.

"This is how it's going to be, Tammy. You will get up early and tend to your mother's needs before school. You'll cook breakfast for us all and come straight home every day to prepare the evening meal and do the housework. After that, homework. You will no longer be part of the drama club or the school choir. It's all about making your mother comfortable, making the house run smoothly. You may remain in the church choir, but that's it. Do you understand?"

She nodded, her eyes still flashing resentment. "I would have done it anyway. I would do anything for Mom."

"Than be a good daughter, so she doesn't have to worry about the house or us. Your brothers can look after the garden and take out the trash."

He stood up, feeling the weight of the world on his shoulders. "I'm going into my office, and I don't want to be disturbed." He looked at Tammy again. "Your mother is sleeping, so let her rest."

"I won't disturb her, Dad. I just want to sit with her."

"There's no point if she's not awake."

Tammy's face crumpled. "Please. *Please*, Dad."

Danny suddenly realized that he, at last, had something to hold over his daughter. If Tammy didn't toe the line, he would simply threaten to withhold time with her mother. He kept his face stern while letting the seconds stretch out and then nodded and pointed a finger. "Half an hour. You don't talk. You just sit. And if I have any indication that you're not pulling your weight, you don't get to go in there apart from taking care of her basic needs. Understand?"

For a second, hatred flashed in her eyes, but she ground out a reply. "Yes."

"Yes, Dad."

"Yes, Dad."

For the implied insolence, he almost withdrew tonight's privilege, but he let it go.

She would keep.

"Do the washing up first," he said. "Your mother likes a clean kitchen. Keep it that way. Garrett and Kyle, I want to see you in my office for a few moments."

Rules needed to be established with all his children, but Tammy didn't need to be a party to what he would share with her brothers.

4

Aunt Nat

Three Weeks Later

ALMOST SEVEN HUNDRED MILES AWAY, in Chesterfield, Missouri, Natalie Arnold slung her sports bag containing her guns over her shoulder and double-checked that the slow cooker was on low. She was about to step through the front door when the phone rang.

Nat stopped for a moment and listened, waiting to see if whoever it was would leave a message. She was already running a little late for practice, and the last thing she needed was to get caught up with someone who wanted a chat.

It was most likely Molly. Much as she loved her neighbor, that woman could talk.

After six rings, the answering machine cut in, and she heard a young girl's voice, speaking hesitantly. "Aunt Nat? It's—it's Tammy. Um, look, I'll ring you back later, okay? Please don't ring the house, please don't do that. I'll just call you as soon as I can. I don't even know if you're in Chesterfield." Her niece's voice trembled. "Um, okay, talk soon—"

As soon as Nat heard '…please don't ring the house', she dropped her bag and raced to the phone, snatching it up just as Tammy was about to hang up. She'd known this day would come. What had that cold-hearted fish done now?

"Tammy? I'm here. You just caught me."

"Oh, Aunt Nat." Tammy's voice broke, relief mixed with anguish. *"Aunt Nat."*

"What's wrong?" Apprehension made Nat's voice sharp, but when she heard herself, she immediately softened it. "Tams…?"

There was a soft hitch in the girl's breath and a few almost inaudible sounds that clearly showed Tammy was trying to gain control of herself. "Everything," she finally said. "Just…everything. Aunt Nat, can you come? He'll be mad, but Mom wants you."

"Of course I can. Yes. But Tammy, sweetie, what's wrong?"

"Mom…." Another silence, then: "Aunt Nat, she's… really sick. She's dying. And Dad's making me look after Mom and the house, but he hardly lets me in the room to see her when he's home, and she keeps asking for you, and Dad won't—won't…."

Hearing Tammy as though through a fog, Nat sank into the armchair by the phone. She gripped the receiver hard, her heart thumping. Susannah, her sweet, foolish little sister, dying?

"Aunt Nat?"

"I'm here." Forcing herself to keep a level voice, to project the calmness that the child needed, she said,

"I'm so sorry. What's making her sick, Tammy? What is it?"

"Cancer."

That one word hung in the air between them for a moment, and Nat blinked back tears.

"Cancer," she said. "How long has she been sick?"

"A couple of months. She wasn't feeling well, and then she went to the doctor, and then to the hospital for tests, then… they let her come home. Three weeks ago."

"I see." Her mind raced, sorting through the implications. She wanted to ask how much time Susannah had left, but Tammy might not know, and it seemed cruel. "Who's looking after her when you're at school, Tammy?"

"Some ladies from the church take it in turns. Then yesterday the lady who was going to come phoned to say she'd had an accident on the way and asked me to call someone else, but I stayed home from school instead. Aunt Nat…" her voice broke. "She's so sick. And she talks about you a lot."

Fury rushed through her, pure and undiluted hatred for Danny Dyson and his selfish ways. How could he not allow Susannah to tell her only sister that she was dying? Knowing Dyson, she would probably have got nothing more than an abrupt phone call to let her know the time of her sister's funeral if he told her at all.

Tammy's panicked voice sounded again. "Aunt Nat, I have to go. Marie from the church is coming down the driveway, and they can't know I phoned you."

"Don't worry, sweetie. I'm coming, right? I'll pretend I'm on the way home from a competition, and I'm just calling in for a quick visit. He won't know."

"Thank you. *Thank you.* I've got to go."

Nat was left staring at the phone in her hand, fighting tears of grief and shock.

That poor little girl.

She'd need a friend in that household, with her cold father and those nasty brothers swaggering around.

Nat swiped a hand across her eyes, replaced the phone in the dock, and went to her bedroom to pack.

5

Salvation

NAT PREPARED her cover story carefully. Houston, she decided; that's where she'd say she'd been for the past few weeks. It was nearly eight hundred miles from Chesterfield, but only a four-hour drive from Baton Rouge, so it was logical that she'd make a surprise visit to her little sister Susannah.

She wouldn't say she'd been in a competition, she thought, in case Danny Dyson was suspicious enough to follow up and saw there was no competition listed. Instead, her story would be that she had agreed to help train some up-and-coming shooters in skeet and clay on the Houston range for a couple of weeks.

That would give her reason to pack more clothes— enough to stay as long as Susannah needed her, no matter what Danny Dyson had to say about it. The anger curled through her again.

He had women coming in from the church and poor little Tammy battling to cope when Susannah's own sister was perfectly capable of doing it?

She made a few quick calls to the club, called in to let Molly down the road know she'd be away, and set off within the hour, covering 450 miles for the day. She was careful to take breaks and stay alert before deciding enough was enough and pulling up at a roadside motel just after dark. As she had expected, she tossed and turned most of the night, thinking of Susannah and what a tragedy it had been, getting caught up with a man like Danny Dyson. But there had been no reasoning with little sister.

Nat had never liked him, but young Susannah had been dazzled.

Dyson first laid eyes on Nat's sister in the church, singing a solo in her pure voice and looking like an angel in a simple white dress with that soft blonde hair and huge blue eyes. From that moment, Danny had been bound and determined to have her. Handsome, charming Danny Dyson, already an influential figure in the church and eight years older than Susannah.

Her little sister didn't stand a chance.

He'd pretended to make Nat welcome the few times she had come to visit when Susannah had had the babies, but they could all sense the tension. Susannah was sad that her beloved Danny and her big sister didn't get on, but she looked forward to her rare visits anyway. She was proud of Nat, the winner of all those trophies, and was devastated when she missed out on Olympic team selection by a whisker.

Even so, Susannah hated guns and couldn't understand Nat's fascination with them. All she wanted was for Nat to be as happily married as she was, with children of her own.

She was utterly blind to Danny's faults, Nat knew. As

far as Susannah was concerned her Danny could do no wrong, no matter what her parents or Nat said. Bit by bit, Danny had succeeded in putting distance between Susannah and her family while pretending that they were always welcome. There was always a reason why Susannah couldn't come to visit them. In the end, they gave up and resigned themselves to token visits.

The next day, Nat was on the road again early and reached Baton Rouge that afternoon, glazed with fatigue and worry and aching after driving for two days in a car without decent lumbar support.

Rest, she told herself firmly.

Susannah and Tammy would need her fresh and ready to cope with anything. Tomorrow morning, she'd wait until mid-morning to give credence to her story that she'd driven from Houston.

Tammy and the boys should be at school and Danny at work. She aimed to talk to the ladies from the church and assess the situation before they all got home.

The woman who answered the door was about eight inches shorter than Nat, small and neat and capable in her plaid cotton shirt and knee-length shorts. Her short pepper-and-salt hair was pulled back off her face into a stubby ponytail, and she had a tea towel slung over one shoulder. It was hot, and beads of sweat showed at her hairline.

"Good morning," she said with a polite smile.

"Hi," Nat said, gearing herself up to play a part that would not get Tammy into trouble. "Is Susannah here?"

A tiny frown appeared on the other woman's forehead. "She's here, but she's not seeing visitors. She's... not well."

"She's not?" Nat let her own forehead crease in concern and puzzlement. "She hasn't said anything." She extended a hand. "I'm her sister, Nat. From Chesterfield."

"Nat... Natalie? You must be the one that has been overseas. So you're back? Susannah will be so happy." A sweet smile lit her face as she shook Nat's hand, and then she added belatedly, "I'm Grace. I'm one of the women from the church. We have a roster to look after her, helping out poor Danny."

Overseas? thought Nat, making a heroic effort to keep the anger from showing on her face. So that had been Danny's story?

She focused on Grace's words. "A roster, you said?" She frowned. "Just how sick is my sister?"

"This is awkward," Grace said. She shook her head. "What am I doing, keeping you here on the doorstep? Come in, sit down." She stepped back and led the way into the family room off the kitchen, putting a finger to her lips and inclining her head in the direction of the bedrooms, lowering her voice. "She's not long taken her meds, and she's sleeping."

From a quick assessment of the woman sitting in the lounge chair opposite her, Nat had decided that Grace looked like the down-to-earth type. One who would call it as it was. She'd find out as much as she could before Tammy and the boys came home from school.

"When did you get back from Europe?" Grace asked.

Go along with it, for now, Nat told herself, biting

back the impulse to tell Grace that Danny, that fine upstanding church elder, couldn't tell the truth if he tried.

"Not long ago," she said. "I've been in Houston for the past couple of weeks, training a team in clay and skeet, and I thought I'd surprise Susannah before I went back home. So here I am." She let her concern show. "Grace, can you do me a favor and be honest with me about my sister? I need to know exactly what's wrong."

"Oh, dear. I'm so sorry." As she had predicted, Grace sat up straighter and gave it to her straight, empathetic but sensible. "She's got aggressive ovarian cancer, Natalie." Pity filled her eyes, but her voice remained steady. "I'm afraid it's terminal."

"Nat. Call me Nat." She focused on staying calm. "And my parents—they don't know?"

"Danny thought it best to keep it from them as long as possible, since they're old and frail, and it's a long trip from their retirement home." Grace glanced away for a moment, her lips firming. It seemed she wasn't entirely convinced that it was a good idea to keep Susannah's parents in the dark.

Old and frail indeed. Her parents had been older than most when they had their children, true, and were now in their late seventies, but they weren't so feeble that they couldn't be told about a dying daughter.

"What about me? He thought it best I shouldn't know, either?" This time, she let her anger show—just a little.

"He said…." Grace looked a little embarrassed and glanced away for a moment. "I think he thought he was doing the right thing. Trying to think of what was best for everyone. He said because you were overseas, in training for competition at a high level, they shouldn't worry you… until Susannah's last days."

Nat closed her eyes for a moment. *Keep your cool.* The most important thing was to stay here. If she exposed Danny Dyson for what he was, he'd kick her out. She had no rights here.

"Grace…." She swallowed. "*Nothing* is more important to me than looking after my sister. And what about Tammy and my nephews? How are they coping?"

"Tammy." Grace's eyes softened. "That little girl is a trouper. As sweet as Susannah, but with a bit more steel in her. I've been worried about her, to tell you the truth. She loves her Mom, but she's carrying too much for a thirteen-year-old. It's good that you're here. The boys—well, Garrett is a wonderful boy; we all love him. He's just like his mother and sister. Kyle does what he can to help, but he's working with his Uncle Rocky a lot now."

Nat didn't miss the faint hint of disapproval when Marie mentioned Rocky's name, but she filed that away for later. She sat forward in her seat. "Grace, I need to know as much as possible before Susannah wakes and the kids get home. Tell me about the routine, the meds… and what you need to do for my sister." She gave her a bleak smile. "I can see that the women from the church have been lifesavers, but I'm here now."

"We'll all still be here to help," Grace assured her. "But little Tammy, she's the one we've been worried about. Danny says it's character-forming, making her step up, but… she's breaking, I can tell. Danny is doing the best he can, but he's not seeing things straight."

"Go on."

So Grace did. By the time they heard Susannah's soft voice call out, almost an hour later, Nat was barely keeping a cap on her anger.

Nothing was going to get her out of this house as long as her sister was alive.

6

Confrontation

DANNY DYSON WAS FUMING.

He'd called into the church to drop off some paperwork and had run into Grace Tennant, who was supposed to be looking after his wife, only to find that his sister-in-law had turned up and sent Grace home.

Natalie Arnold, that impossible woman, whom he'd gone to so much trouble to keep at a distance. Hiding his irritation from Grace, Danny had pretended to be surprised and delighted that Natalie was back from Europe.

"Isn't it wonderful?" Grace said, clutching his arm. "You must be so relieved. Now our Susannah can have her family around her and take some of the load off little Tammy."

He smiled at her, putting on his brave-husband face. He'd always been able to charm the church women, and Grace was far from immune. "I had no idea she was back in the country—but that's our Natalie, so caught up in her guns and competitions that she can lose track of family." He managed to inject just the faintest note of censure in his voice when he said 'guns', knowing Grace's opinion of firearms and violence in today's society, and followed it up with pretended concern. "How did she take the news? She and Susannah were very close as children."

Grace's face sobered. "She was upset, as you can imagine. Apparently, she got back a few weeks ago, and she's been in Houston, doing some kind of training. She just popped into Baton Rouge for a few days to catch up with Susannah, and it was a terrible shock to hear the bad news."

"I can imagine."

So, Natalie hadn't blown his cover story. After processing that information for a split second, he could guess why. She wanted to stay, to be a part of Susannah's last days, and if she picked a fight with him, she had no chance.

Every part of him rebelled at the thought of her staying. On the other hand, he couldn't risk alienating any of the church community. He'd think of something. Meanwhile, he needed to get to Tammy before Nat saw her and warn her about what she could and couldn't tell her aunt.

"Grace, I owe you and the others a tremendous debt for what you've already done," he said. "But I need to ask...." He stopped for a moment as though reluctant to continue. "I'm glad that Natalie has turned up, but she's... well, let me just be charitable and say she's not always reliable. May I call on you again if we need you?"

Immediately he knew he'd played it wrong. Something changed in her eyes, and she drew back, just a fraction.

"Perhaps she's changed," Grace said, still smiling but with a hint of reserve. "She says that Susannah is the most important thing in her life right now, and she'll be here as long as she's needed. I didn't get the impression that she might leave… but then, you know her; I don't."

"If she has matured at last into the fine woman I always thought she could be," he said earnestly, "I'll be the happiest man in the world. Susannah always told me that Natalie would come good." He allowed just a hint of moisture to enter his eyes, and Grace immediately warmed to him again.

She squeezed his hand. "You just go on home to your family, Danny. Marie and I will still be there for an hour or two most days to help with housework or to sit with Susannah so Nat can take a break. I'm sure it will all work out. God is good, and we all know He works in mysterious ways."

"Indeed he does." He lifted a hand in farewell and, with a sad smile, went on his way.

The moment he was in his car, he slammed a fist on the steering wheel and closed his eyes tight, holding in what he really wanted to say.

Danny Dyson did not cuss.

He breathed deeply for several minutes, willing the rage to die down, before carefully turning the key in the ignition and heading for home. He should just about beat the school bus.

Tammy stepped off the bus, aware of Garrett just behind her, and felt her shoulders hunch. She didn't look at Kyle, who was leaning against the fence waiting for them. In just a few minutes, all three of them would all be out of sight of the road, heading up the drive to the house.

She could tell that Garrett was in one of his moods, and Kyle would follow where he led. Probably nobody but she would even realize Garrett was out of sorts, because he was careful to maintain his laid-back, good-guy image to pretty much everyone. Most people had no idea what he was capable of because Garrett was a genius at getting payback in devious ways.

"Move it along, Tammy," he said softly, practically treading on her heels. "You've got things to do, remember. No time for slacking off." He ruffled her hair in what would look like an affectionate gesture to anyone looking back from the departing bus, but he took care to thread his fingers through and yank hard before he moved away, opening the gate for her with an inviting sweep of his hand.

Kyle's eyes flicked from Garrett to Tammy, and he grinned, standing back and waiting for her to go ahead.

Tammy gritted her teeth and went forward with her head down, not letting her fear show. Any sign of weakness made Garrett worse.

Then they heard the familiar growl of an approaching car, and for once in her life, Tammy was relieved to turn and see her father at the wheel. He waited while Garrett opened the gate wider so he could drive through, but he didn't continue up the driveway. Instead, he rolled down the window and said tightly, "Get in."

Tammy wanted to run. Far, far away. First Garrett, now her father, whose behavior was equally unpredictable when he was mad about something. He didn't physically hurt her, like Garrett, but his words could be even more scathing than his youngest son's.

When they were all in the car, he looked at Garrett and then back at her, sitting tensely in the back seat, as far away from Kyle as she could get. "Did any of you contact your Aunt Natalie?"

She's here. The rush of relief almost left Tammy breathless, but she was so scared it was an effort not to tremble. Did he know? Did he suspect? Unable to speak, she simply shook her head.

"Not me," Garrett said. "I don't even like her."

Kyle groaned. "Not *her*."

"That'll be enough," his father said brusquely. "She's family; you'll show respect."

"Sorry, Father." Garrett looked over his shoulder at Tammy, but he didn't seem suspicious, although he momentarily narrowed his eyes at her. "Why? Is she coming to stay?"

"She is, I believe, already here." A muscle jumped in his father's jaw. "So Grace Tennant tells me."

Garrett rolled his eyes but said nothing more.

"You tell her as little as possible." Her father pointed at Tammy, the eyes that could twinkle with charm and good humor now cold and threatening. "No need to play the martyr and make a big deal of everything you've been doing for your mother. That's family business. *Our* family, not including your aunt. Clear?"

Tammy nodded.

"If I hear one word from Natalie Arnold about you being overburdened or mistreated, she's out of here. If she gives me any lip at all, she's out." He paused and then added, "And if I catch you spending too much time with her, she'll be gone. Understand?"

"Yes," Tammy managed, the word sticking in her throat.

She hated him. *Hated him.*

"When you speak with her, remember that I was under the clear impression she was busy training in Europe and had no wish to interfere with that. I thought it could wait until… well, until the end was near."

Stunned at such a bald-faced lie, Tammy found her voice at last. "Mom was surprised to hear she was overseas." She knew she shouldn't continue, but the words seemed to spill out of their own volition. "We should have tried to contact her."

Her father stabbed a finger at her. "I did what I thought was best for your mother. She's very, very sick. She's dying. What does it take to get it through your head? The last thing she needs is that headstrong elder sister of hers here stirring things up, but now it's too late." He turned to stare at the driveway, curving around out of sight through the trees, as though trying to see the house half a mile away.

Tammy watched while he breathed deeply, his fingers clenched on the wheel, until his shoulders relaxed and his face smoothed out. She'd seen him do this before, and it scared her almost as much as his cold words and bitter rejection.

Her father was assuming his benign, caring mask, ready to confront her Aunt Nat and pretend to be welcoming.

When she looked at Garrett, he was also watching his father, a slight smile tugging at his lips.

Psycho son and psycho father.

Garrett had learned from a master.

She hoped her Aunt Nat could carry it off.

7

Danny's Plan

Nat had been expecting Tammy and Garrett to arrive on foot after catching the bus home, so she was caught unawares when she heard the sound of a car coming up the drive.

Danny, she thought, instinctively squaring her shoulders and preparing for the confrontation. After he'd gone to such extremes to keep the news of his wife's illness from her, he wouldn't be happy to see her.

The sound of a car door slamming made Susannah open her eyes. She glanced at the bedside clock and smiled, squeezing her sister's hand. "Is that Danny? He's home early… and the children will be here any minute too," she said, her soft voice content. "They'll be so surprised to see you!"

"I'm sure they will," Nat said, her heart rate rising. She wasn't afraid of Danny, but she would have to take care.

The front door opened, and they heard footsteps approaching the bedroom. Then Danny was there, standing in the doorway, his eyes going immediately to Nat.

"Danny!" Susannah said warmly. "Look who's here!"

A wide, delighted smile grew on Danny's face as he looked at Nat. "I know, darling. I ran into Grace, and she told me that your sister had come to visit." He moved to Nat's side and bent to give her a brotherly buss on the cheek. "It's wonderful that you're here. Even though I'm sure you'll have to get back to your training, a few days of your company will do Susannah a world of good." He leaned over his wife, kissed her on the forehead, and smoothed her hair back from her forehead. "How are you feeling, darling?"

"Better than I have for days," she said, her eyes filled with happiness. "Seeing Nat here when I woke up was better than any medicine."

"And the good news is," Nat said, "I can stay as long as Susannah wants me here."

Susannah couldn't stop smiling. "Isn't that wonderful, Danny?"

"Wonderful," he echoed, straightening up, his smiling eyes meeting Nat's. "But what about your training? Won't months out of the circuit harm your chances?"

"Not a problem," Nat said coolly. "Now that I'm back from overseas, I'm free to do what I want."

"I had no idea you were back," he responded, his face innocent. "When the young man who answered the phone at your club said you weren't in the country, I was thrown for a loop. But Susannah and I talked it over, and we agreed that you didn't need to know for a while yet. We know how important your guns are to you."

Sensitive to the slur, Nat gritted her teeth. Guns weren't important to her. The skill, precision, and challenge of the competition were, but he'd never understood that. She zeroed in on his other statement and asked, keeping her expression neutral, "Who was it that told you I was out of the country?"

He shrugged, making a dismissive motion. "No idea. Some young fellow. Sounded in a bit of a hurry. I didn't get a name—you'll understand that my mind was on Susannah at the time."

"Of course." Nat smiled at him. "It's not important, anyway, is it? What is important is that I'm here, and I'm staying. You concentrate on work, and Susannah when you're not at work, and I'll make sure things run smoothly in the house when you're not here. Sound like a deal?"

That should make it clear enough that she planned to stay.

For a split second, something feral flashed behind the good humor in his eyes, so brief that she might think she had imagined it if she hadn't been watching for it. To the casual observer, his expression would not have changed. "That's so generous of you, Natalie. Are you sure?"

"Susannah is my only sister. There's no question."

Throughout their conversation, she had been aware of Tammy in the background, standing silently in the doorway with Garrett at her shoulder. Now she finally allowed herself to look at her niece and smile. "Hello, Tammy. How are you doing?"

"Well, thank you, Aunt Nat." The girl gave a shaky smile before looking nervously at her father.

His lips tightened for an instant, then he said, "I've

been sleeping in the guest room so Susannah can get more rest. Tammy can fetch the inflatable mattress from the shed and make it up for you on the floor of her room. I'm afraid you'll have to share her closet."

And just like that, it was done.

Both she and Danny knew that there had been no phone call to the gun club, no young fellow with some story about her being out of the country. But she had no way of proving it, and she didn't care. She was in—and as long as she stayed in the background, she would remain.

Natalie Arnold hadn't risen to the top of her chosen sport without knowing how to play politics.

While Tammy helped her aunt move her things out of the car and rearranged her room to squeeze the two of them in, Danny Dyson called his sons into his office.

"Sit there," he said, pointing to the two-seater sofa that Susannah had chosen carefully to go with the other furniture in the room.

His office was an addition to the house. Eight years before, Susannah had said firmly, "You need a proper office, Danny." Her eyes shone when she told him her idea. "You can't be taking people into the sitting room all the time, not when you've got private things to talk about. It's so hard to keep the children quiet. You've got all those people from the church you counsel. What do you think?"

Danny had been mulling over a similar idea himself. Still, it was typical of his sweet Susannah to worry about his welfare. He had kissed her soundly and said, "You're too good to me, that's what I think," and had wasted no time getting construction underway. He let Susannah think it was a strain on their resources, but in reality, he had money put away that could have paid for the room a hundred times over.

It suited him to maintain a particular face for the church community at this phase of his life. The plan had been that one day, when the children were grown, he'd take Susannah away, and they could live the life he deserved.

Now, that would never happen.

Already, he had spent sleepless hours thinking about how his life would change. Plan B: life after Susannah.

He pushed that bleak thought aside and faced his sons.

"Your Aunt Natalie…" he paused, taking a deep breath while he schooled his expression to remain impassive, and then went on. "As you heard, your aunt will be staying with us for as long as she is needed. I expect you to be respectful and to give her any assistance she requires."

The boys looked at each other, and when Garrett turned his eyes back to his father, there was a wariness there. "How long will that be?"

Danny returned his gaze. He saw a lot of himself in his youngest son. He strongly suspected that Garrett knew what he really thought of Natalie Arnold…just as he suspected that Garrett had more than an inkling of some of his father's underground activities.

"I imagine," Danny said flatly, "she'll be here until the funeral."

The word 'funeral' was like a knife to his heart, and

he had to busy himself with some papers on his desk until he regained control.

"Sure, Dad," Garrett said. "Whatever we can do. Right, Kyle?"

Danny glanced up just in time to see Garrett elbow his brother.

"Right," Kyle agreed. "She's bossy, though. I remember from last time she was here." Then he huffed out a humorless laugh. "Bossy to Garrett and me, anyway. She was easy on Tammy."

Yes, Danny thought sourly. She was. "Two months," he said. "The doctor is unwilling to be precise, but that's my guess. After that, your aunt will return home, and Tammy will be forced to toe the line. For now, I need things here to be peaceful. It's all about your mother. Do you understand?"

Both boys nodded, but Garrett wore a faint frown.

Danny focused his attention on the boy. "I will not have your aunt speaking to me about your not cooperating. Or about Tammy being asked to do more than she should. You will do your chores without complaint. No matter what you feel about Tammy being favored over you, this is not the time to speak up. Is that clear?"

For a second, rebellion flashed in Garrett's eyes, but it was followed by comprehension. Garrett was learning that some things were worth waiting for. "Yes, Dad."

After Natalie was gone, Danny thought, Tammy's life would change. Undoubtedly, she wouldn't like it much, but that was life.

8

Trapped

As soon as her aunt moved in and took charge, Tammy felt a huge weight lift from her shoulders. Her heart was still sore because every time she looked at her mother's increasingly gaunt face, she felt despair so deep she thought she might die too. But now, the after-school hours were hers to share with her Mom, while her Aunt Nat took charge of cooking the evening meal and handling her brothers. As adept and practical in the kitchen as she was on the rifle range, her aunt served up good, nourishing food, full of flavor and with enough variety to satisfy both Danny and his sons. Watching her expression when she knew the men couldn't see her, Tammy realized that Aunt Nat was doing what she had to. If she made the men's lives easier, they'd tolerate her presence.

Then, just as she thought she was safe, the bullying after school started again. Her brothers held back for a week, contenting themselves with sly comments about her appearance and intelligence when her aunt was elsewhere. Then the cheerleader that Garrett had been seeing discovered that he was two-timing her with midnight visits to a rival and got her revenge by dumping him very publicly on the front steps of the school.

Tammy, waiting for the bus, had seen it all. Garrett handled it with calculated charm, wit, and pretended sheepishness and somehow ended up with most people on his side, as usual.

But when he saw Tammy watching, trying to make herself invisible at the back of a group of onlookers, his brow lowered, and she knew that she'd pay the price of witnessing such public humiliation.

The moment they were through the gate and out of sight of the main road, with the sound of the school bus retreating into the distance, he grabbed her by the arm, dragged her behind a tree, and shoved her up against it. It was one of his favorite ploys: get out of sight, pin her up against a tree or a shed or a fence so she couldn't escape, and then start in on her. He liked to twist her arm or force back her fingers, forcing her to look at him while his eyes glared into hers. He would tell her that she was worthless and stupid and Mommy's little pet, and one day, she would learn that she couldn't get a free ride through life.

Today, for the first time, he used his whole body to hold her squashed against the tree, using one hand to pin her wrists over her head. The other hand forced up her chin, so she had no choice but to stare at him, shaking with fear. She could feel his breath on her cheek.

He was so *strong*. And he hated her.

"Garrett, please don't. Please. Let me go." Her voice cracked.

Instead, he leaned on her harder. "You loved seeing

Jaimii Miller doing that, didn't you? I could hear you back there, laughing with the others." He forced her chin up higher, so the tendons in her neck stretched unbearably. "Thought it was *funny*."

"I didn't, Garrett. No." And she hadn't even wanted to look; the moment she saw what was happening; saw gorgeous Jamii marching up to him on the steps, with her auburn hair flying in the breeze and her eyes snapping with fury, Tammy had wanted to disappear into a hole.

Wishing she were anywhere but witnessing that.

"Crap. I saw you. Well, now I'll give you something *else* to laugh about." His fingers loosened their grip on her chin and moved to her neck.

"No! Garrett!" Terrified, she struggled.

"*Yes*, Tammy." He squeezed, increasing the pressure bit by bit. The expression in his eyes changed from bitter anger to calculation and cold pleasure.

At that instant, Tammy realized that her brother was truly dangerous.

"I'm…." she couldn't swallow, couldn't breathe. She had to stop him. "Telling Aunt N…" She couldn't get out another syllable, but that was enough to stop him.

The pressure on her neck eased, but his eyes changed again—pure, icy hatred.

"If you tell our aunt," he said, "I'll tell Dad you made it up *again*. Trying to turn Auntie Nat against me. And then he'll make her leave."

Tammy closed her eyes.

If her aunt left, things could only get worse. She and her mother *needed* her aunt.

With her aunt in the house, Tammy could have her afternoons free to be with her Mom. To sing for her, when she was needed something to take her mind off the pain…

Garrett moved his lips close to her ear and whispered silkily, "Do you want our aunt to leave, Tammy?"

She shook her head, and despite herself, a tiny whimper of fear escaped.

"*Look* at me, Tammy."

Nausea rising inside her, she forced her eyes open and stared into the eyes of a psychopath. "No," she croaked.

His voice soft and charming, he said, "Then you say *nothing*. About what happens today, or any other day."

She said nothing, feeling boneless, helpless.

"Say '*yes*', Tammy. *'Yes, Garrett'.*"

"Yes, Garrett."

"Apologize for laughing today."

"I'm sorry for laughing."

"Admit that you deserve to be punished."

She shook her head.

"*Say it!*"

Everything inside her rebelled, but then she thought of her mother and made herself murmur, "I deserve to be punished."

"Good girl." He finally let her go, stood back and looked at her, frowned, and smoothed the back of his fingers down her throat. She quivered at the sensation of his knuckles.

"There's some redness there. Make sure you cover it up before Aunt Nat sees it."

For one wild moment, Tammy thought of disobeying him, pointing to the marks on her throat as proof that what she was saying was true.

Then she realized, bleakly, that it wouldn't work anyway. He'd say she did it to herself to add credence to her story, and her father would be angry as well, and things would get immeasurably worse.

In a split second, she made a decision. When it was all over, she'd run away. Even life on the streets couldn't be worse than this.

He stared at her and pointed at her throat. "Don't even think about telling her."

"All right."

"Not. One. Word."

"All *right*."

Garrett smiled. "Good. Until tomorrow, then."

He let her go and strode off, leaving Tammy to shakily pick up her bag and trudge after him.

It didn't take Nat long to realize that something had happened.

She was chatting softly to Susannah when the front door opened. "The kids are home," Susannah said, her face lighting up as usual. "You know, I think I'll ask Tammy to sing for me this afternoon."

Tammy didn't immediately poke her head around the door as she usually did. They heard the sound of light footsteps going to her room while Garrett's heavier tread went to the bigger bedroom that he shared with Kyle. Then there was the thump of a school backpack hitting the floor in Garrett's room before he came back and walked over to his mother.

"Hi, Mom." He kissed her cheek and smiled, squeezing her hand. "How are you feeling?"

"Just fine," Susannah told him, smiling up at her youngest son. It was her usual response, even if she'd had a bad day. Susannah never complained. "How was your day, darling?"

"Good. I scored a hundred percent in the math exam." He gave a thumbs-up.

"Oh, that's wonderful!" Her smile grew wider. "My clever boy." She turned to Nat, inviting her to comment. "Isn't he amazing, Nat?"

"Amazing," Nat agreed, manufacturing a smile.

Garrett wasn't fooled, but he nodded at her, including her with a warm smile. "Thanks." Then he made a sad face, looking back at his mother. "But Jamii Miller dumped me. Guess I'll just have to find another girlfriend, hey?"

"Jamii dumped *you*?" His mother looked astonished, her blue eyes wide. "Why?"

"No idea." He shrugged nonchalantly. "Has her eye on somebody else, I guess."

"The girl's a fool. She'll regret it." His mother looked past him to the door. "Where's Tammy?"

"In her room, I think. Want me to get her?"

"She usually calls in to say hello the moment she walks through the door. I hope everything's all right at school." Susannah glanced at Nat. "I think she's struggling a bit with all that's going on at home. Danny says her grades are dropping."

Then they heard Tammy's door open, and a moment later, she was there with them.

"Hi, Mom!" Tammy beamed widely, moving to the opposite side of the bed from Garrett and bending over her mother. "You look better today." Like Nat, she celebrated every tiny improvement.

Nat, watching the love in the glances the two exchanged, was struck anew by how much Tammy looked like her mother. From where she stood, she could see the two profiles, one looking up, the other looking down. Two tip-tilted noses; two sets of smiling, full lips. The same blonde hair, the same wide blue eyes.

Tammy was filling out, too, beginning to develop feminine curves. Today, in her teal t-shirt and cropped white pants, Nat could see hints of what her mother had looked like at her age. She loved clothes, just as Susannah did: the filmy teal-and-turquoise scarf tied around her neck picked up the color of her t-shirt.

Every time Tammy looked in a mirror, she would be reminded of her mother.

Nat had to look away at the sudden surge of melancholy.

"I had a lovely day, thank you, darling," Susannah told her daughter, sounding bright. "I've been awake all afternoon, chatting with Nat about old times. We haven't had such a good talk for years." She looked at Tammy hopefully. "Sweetie, do you think you might sing a little for me today?"

Tammy's hand went instinctively to her throat, and she toyed with the scarf. "I'm actually a little croaky today, but I'll try."

Something about the way she said it made Nat look at her again, and then she saw the tension.

Something had happened.

What? Teasing at school? Someone saying the wrong thing about her sick mother?

"Oh, dear. You mustn't sing if you have a sore throat. Do you think you're catching a cold?" Susannah wriggled into a more upright position on the pillows. "Come here, open your mouth and let me see."

"No." Nat and Tammy spoke together, and Tammy stepped back. They both knew the dangers of Susannah being exposed to infection.

Susannah gave an impatient sigh and sank back. "All right."

"I don't think it's a cold," Tammy said. "I had to do a presentation at school, so I've been talking more than usual."

"Oh, darling! Tell me more. What was it about?"

"Just, um, the life cycle of insects." The hesitation before Tammy answered, along with the way she avoided their eyes, told Nat that she was lying. "Not very interesting. No, I *want* to sing, Mom. I'll just have a drink of water first."

"Well, then, I might leave you to it," Garrett said. "All the musical talent went to Tammy, I'm afraid. I'll be doing my homework in my room if anyone needs me."

He left, but Nat didn't miss the swift glance of warning he sent his sister.

What was all *that* about?

She intended to find out.

9

What Will Be, Will Be

TAMMY REALLY DID HAVE a glorious voice, Nat thought, listening to her niece sing one song after another for Susannah. The list was peppered with old favorites that the two of them had sung together over the years: Patsy Cline, Doris Day, Ella Fitzgerald, Shirley Bassey, and a few numbers from Bing Crosby and Neil Diamond thrown in. Nat had learned from her sister that she and Tammy had loved to cuddle up together and watch old movies, and then act out the parts.

Here and there, Susannah joined in the chorus, or Tammy would pause and wait while her mother sang a line or two, both of them exchanging special smiles.

Memories, Nat thought, choking back unaccustomed tears. They were tapping into memories of fun days dressing up and singing songs from old movies together… and making new memories that Tammy could cling to after her mother was gone.

Tammy was the one to call a halt, seeing the all-too-familiar vertical crease between Susannah's eyes that signaled pain.

"You're tired, Mom." She took her mother's hand and kissed her on the cheek. "That's enough for now."

"One more. Just one, sweetheart."

Tammy hesitated, exchanging a quick look with Nat, and then agreed. "Okay. Last request of the day. What's it to be?"

"One of my all-time favorites." Susannah's eyes grew serious, the sadness in the depths all too obvious. "One that has new meaning for us now, sweetie. We never know what life brings us, Tammy, but I know it's going to bring all good things for you. I *know* it. Keep looking forward, darling girl."

Tammy's eyes glistened at the reminder that her mother wouldn't be with her much longer, but she held it together and kept smiling, holding on to her hand. "It'll be our special song, then. Which one?"

"*Que Sera Sera*," Susannah said and smiled up at her. "What will be, will be. Remember that, Tams: the future is not ours to see."

Tammy's lower lip trembled, but she nodded and took a deep breath. "Our song."

While the sweet, sad strains of the song echoed through the room, Nat got up and walked softly out of the door, leaving them together.

This moment was just for Tammy and her Mom.

10

Caught

For the next few days, Natalie Arnold kept her ears and eyes open. She especially watched the interaction between Tammy and Garrett and filed away every meaningful glance, every mood.

She learned more about Garrett, and increasingly, she didn't like what she saw. Most of the time, the boy appeared easy-going, amusing, and amenable. He cheerfully did whatever she asked of him, was gentle and sweet with his mother, and treated Tammy with the kind of tolerant affection that you would expect between a good-natured, popular athlete and his kid sister. His brother Kyle hung off his every word, and his father's gaze always softened when he looked at Garrett.

And Susannah glowed with pride and love whenever he came to see her.

The golden boy.

However, Nat knew at a bone-deep level that Garrett was not who he appeared. She recalled from brief visits over the years that when the boy was a lot younger, his teasing had sometimes had his younger sister in tears.

He was always contrite—or aggrieved, depending on the circumstances—but there was *something* there.

And however lightly he dismissed young Jamii Miller breaking up with him, she sensed simmering anger, deep below the surface.

For the next few days, she made a practice of hovering for a moment near the door after she left a room, listening. Almost every time, Garrett waited a few moments and then said something in an undertone that elicited a muffled response from Tammy. Once, Nat picked up Tammy murmuring a submissive "Yes, Garrett," and another time she heard the girl's voice, quivering with apprehension, saying: "Nothing, Garrett. *Nothing*. Honestly." That was followed by a hushed warning from Garrett to keep her voice down and a barely audible "Sorry" from Tammy.

Nat silently moved away, trying to guess what Tammy had meant. That she had *done* nothing—or *said* nothing? Mulling over it, she came to the conclusion that the only place Garrett would drop his nice-boy facade was when he could be sure there would be nobody eavesdropping.

That meant either on the way to school, at school, or on the way home.

The next afternoon, Susannah was still sleeping peacefully twenty minutes before the school bus was due to drop the kids off, so Nat slipped out and headed for the grove of trees halfway along the driveway. There, she figured, she could hide and watch the two of them to see if her suspicions were correct. Now that she was here, Kyle spent most days at his Uncle Rocky's farm. Sometimes his father drove him; sometimes, his uncle picked him up. He usually timed his return in the after-noons to coincide with his brother's.

Several trees at the back of the grove were in the midst of a tangle of shrubs. Nat's keen eye, practiced from many hours on the rifle range, assessed distances and angles, and figured that if she squatted there, she would be able to catch a glimpse of the bus approaching and also be able to see most of the driveway, right up to the house. She should be able to follow the kids and listen, slipping from tree to tree for cover.

What she witnessed had her clenching her teeth in a rage.

Thinking he was unobserved, Garrett started on his sister the moment the bus was out of sight. He seized Tammy's long blonde hair and tugged on it to force her head back and then herded her along the driveway in front of him, saying something in a low voice. He kept it up until they moved past her, and Nat caught the words "…on the bathroom door. My *sister*, innocent little Tammy. How many boys have you given your phone number to, Tammy?"

"I haven't," she said, her voice desolate. "You know I haven't, Garrett."

"I bet you have a list of names. And money from boys. Where are you hiding it?" He stopped her and stared into her eyes while he asked.

"I don't! I'm not!" She tried to pull away from him, which incensed him further. He grabbed her by both arms and shook her, hauling her off into the trees where they couldn't be seen.

Just a dozen steps from Nat's vantage point.

"Don't deny it," he said, his voice soft but filled with menace. "I'm going to search your room, find it. Money, names. Show it all to Dad so he can ask where you got it. What do you think *he* will say?" He held her, back against a tree, with one strong hand on her shoulder and the other holding up her school bag. He shook it. "Maybe there's something in here? I'd better check."

"Please, don't."

Nat's heart bled for the girl, but she remained hidden, thinking fast.

The boy had to be stopped. To do that, she needed evidence. She needed a camera, and hers was back in her room.

Next time, she'd have it with her. And since she'd treated herself to a ridiculously expensive new digital camera on her last birthday, she wouldn't have to wait for photos to be developed.

The evidence would be right there...on the camera and backed up to her computer.

She watched, and listened, and learned a lot while Garrett was entertaining himself, emptying out the contents of Tammy's bag onto the dirt before he ordered her to pick it all up again.

"I'll have to search your room, Tammy," he said. "When you're in with Mom this afternoon. I'll find anything you've hidden."

"You can't," she said shakily. "It's Aunt Nat's room too."

"I can do what I want. I'll find out if *she's* hiding anything too, won't I?"

Finally seeming to tire of the game, he pointed to the driveway and then dogged her footsteps all the way home, while Tammy resolutely kept her head down, putting one slow foot in front of the other until she reached safety. The moment the house came in view,

Garrett stepped up beside her and started chatting cheerfully about school and football.

In case his aunt was watching them approach, no doubt.

Nat breathed deeply in an effort to overcome her anger and disgust, weighing up the fallout of any action she might take. Reluctantly, she admitted to herself that speaking to Danny Dyson about Garrett might not end well. Danny clearly had little time for his daughter, whereas he thought the sun shone from Garrett.

If Garrett had succeeded in pulling the wool over his parents' eyes for years, they'd listen if he pleaded extenuating circumstances because of his mother's terminal illness. Danny, already barely tolerant of his sister-in-law, would undoubtedly choose to back his son. What if he used the confrontation as a reason to send her away?

She *couldn't* leave Tammy in this house without anyone in her corner.

No, she decided. Not Danny. Instead, she would confront Garrett, gambling that he was too invested in his good-boy facade to risk exposure. The most important thing right now was to buy time. She had to work out what she was going to do about her niece after Susannah died.

Her mind turned to how she might persuade Garrett to leave his sister alone. She knew instinctively that some form of blackmail would work with a boy like him, but she didn't have time to find something.

That left intimidation, and since he was already bigger and stronger than her, she'd need something else.

Reluctantly, she thought about her guns.

To Nat, firearms were an integral part of her chosen sport. She had never aimed one at a living creature and never intended to. To a boy like him, a gun would represent control.

So… she'd use what she had.

Danny Dyson had reluctantly given permission for Nat to set up a few targets, well away from the house, so she could practice. She'd deliberately asked him in front of Susannah, knowing he couldn't refuse without seeming ungrateful for the way Nat had put her life on hold to help out.

Nat used the makeshift range for an hour or so each day, when one of the ladies from the church arrived to help clean and wash between ten and midday. Danny had insisted that they continue to come each day, pointing out that they were Susannah's friends and she'd want to see them. They always took a break from their duties to sit with her for half an hour or so, chatting and bringing news of the parish, or just sitting quietly if Susannah was tired.

That one hour a day helped Nat to clear her head and re-focus. She felt back in control, with everything narrowing down to wind conditions and reflexes and tactics.

Tactics.

After considering her options, Nat decided what to do.

11

Threats

ON FRIDAY OF THAT WEEK, two days after she'd taken a dozen incriminating photos, Natalie Arnold slid her target pistol into its holster, left the house, and walked past the trees that lined the driveway to the grove of trees. There, she waited behind the usual tree, her camera ostentatiously slung around her neck, ready to hunker down out of sight the moment she saw the school bus approaching.

Kyle's uncle's pickup cruised along a few hundred yards behind the bus. He pulled over, and Kyle jumped out, waved goodbye, and went to join Garrett. Nat noted the grinning glances the boys exchanged as they urged Tammy ahead of them through the gate.

Tammy put her chin in the air and walked away from them, but it didn't take them long to catch up. Watching while the all-too-familiar scene played out, Nat put a lid on her anger and thought about what she was about to do.

This time, at a nod from Garrett, it was Kyle who

urged Tammy off the path. It was like watching a mouse being toyed with by two big cats.

But then the script changed.

This time, the moment Garrett put his hand on his sister, Nat stepped out of hiding and walked steadily toward them. Tammy saw her first, over the boys' shoulders, and her big blue eyes filled with a mixture of shame and relief.

Garrett, seeing his sister's expression change, turned to look.

An eerie calm descended over Nat. It was like being in a competition: once the main show started, her nerves disappeared. It was all about tactics and accuracy, and cool resolve.

"What's this about, Garrett?" she asked mildly, watching while his eyes moved over her and registered the pistol at her hip. "You shouldn't be treating your little sister like that."

He turned around fully, an easy grin coming to his face. "It's just teasing, Aunt Nat. We didn't mean any harm."

His eyes flicked to Kyle with an unmistakable message, and Kyle smirked. He couldn't hide the meanness in his eyes as he backed up his brother. "Just a bit of fun."

"Oh?" Nat said. She smiled back, and then her eyes went to Tammy, who was still standing there with her back against the tree, looking too scared to move. "What do you think, Tammy? Are *you* having fun?"

Garrett didn't look at Tammy, but in the periphery of her vision, Nat saw a slight movement as he nudged his sister's shoe.

Tammy said nothing for a moment and then sighed and spoke softly. "It's all right, Aunt."

Nat switched her gaze to Garret. She simply arched an eyebrow, telegraphing disbelief.

He met her eyes unflinchingly for a few seconds before looking away. He sneaked a sideways glance at Kyle and then stared at the ground before speaking again.

"All right." Garrett sounded frustrated and a little shamefaced. "I'm sorry. Tammy, I had no right to take it out on you. But really, you have to stop it, right? Enough is enough." He cast his sister a halfway-repentant glance before taking a step toward Nat. "You know Jaimii Miller dumped me, right?"

Nat nodded, watching him dig himself a deeper hole.

"Well…" he swallowed and looked away before continuing, "Fact is, although I pretended it didn't matter, it *did*. But Tammy, she's been making jokes about it all week. To me and to the others, so my friends could hear. And…today, I just cracked. I'm *really* sorry."

He turned and opened out his hands helplessly while he looked at his sister. "Here's the deal, Tams. You stop with the jokes, and we'll agree to let bygones be bygones."

Now that he was turned away from her, Nat couldn't see his face, but she could imagine the threatening look that Tammy was getting.

Tammy's gaze skittered away from her brother. Without looking at her aunt, she nodded and said tonelessly, "All right."

Garrett moved toward her, slung an arm around her shoulders, and gave her a playful tap on the forehead.

"All right. All over, then." He picked up her school bag and handed it to her.

"Not quite," Nat said. "I think Kyle should apologize, too. Unless Tammy was making jokes about *his* girlfriend dumping him?"

Kyle's eyebrows lowered, and he glared at her, but then Garrett nodded at him. "She's right. Apologize, Kyle."

Kyle grunted out an ungracious "Sorry," without even looking at his sister.

"Tammy," Nat said, "come over here to me."

Garrett started to walk away, but Nat held up a hand to stop him. "Just a moment, Garrett, please."

Looking as though she might burst into tears at any moment, Tammy moved away from her brothers, closer to her aunt. She stared at the ground.

"Tammy," Nat said softly, "is Garrett telling the truth?"

Garrett gave a theatrical double-take at the question, throwing his arms into the air.

Tammy saw it too. Without looking at her aunt, she gave a tiny nod.

"See?" Garrett said. "Aunt, I know I did the wrong thing, but I *am* telling the truth. I was provoked. I'm not proud of my behavior, but—"

"Garrett," Nat said, "Shut your mouth."

Stunned into silence, he stared at her.

"Tammy, I *know* he has threatened you," Nat said. "I know you're too scared to admit it. But you don't have to keep it a secret any longer, all right?"

Tammy's head snapped up, and she moved the extra few steps to her aunt's side and grabbed her by the arm. "You can't say anything. You can't, or he'll tell Dad, and Dad will make you leave. You *can't* leave."

"No," Nat said. "I won't leave. Because you're not safe, are you, little one?"

Garrett closed his eyes and sighed in frustration. "*Threatened* her? This is ridiculous. Of course, she's safe, Aunt. I wouldn't really hurt her; Tams knows that."

"You're a lying little toad," Nat said evenly. "I've suspected for a while that you might be bullying your sister, Garrett." Her eyes moved to Kyle. "*And* you. You joined in willingly enough today."

"Don't judge me by today, please," Garrett said, his clear blue eyes looking pained. Honesty radiated from him. "I'd do anything to take it back. Tams is my *sister.*"

"Yes," Nat agreed, "unfortunately for her, she is."

Kyle couldn't keep quiet any longer. "Tell Dad, Garrett. Tell him to kick her out, her and her stupid *guns*. He doesn't like her anyway. Those women from the church can do what she does."

"The church women," Nat said. "Such nice ladies. We've become very friendly while we've been looking after your mother." She patted the camera hanging around her neck. "I'm sure they'd be devastated to see the photos I have here."

Garrett's eyes grew cold. At last, he seemed to realize that his act wasn't working. "Photos?"

"Yes," Nat said. "Photos. All this week, except on football training days, I've been right here. Watching and taking photos, and listening." She pointed to the tree. "Seems to be your favorite tree, that one. Tammy can't get away from you when you slam her up against that, can she? Oh, and that one over there." She indicated a different tree, a little further from the road. "That was…let me see… Wednesday."

Garrett took a few steps towards her. "I don't believe you. Let me see them."

Nat's hand slid down to rest on her gun. "So you can take the camera and destroy the evidence? I don't think so. I've made copies, anyway, Garrett. I don't trust you, you see."

His eyes flicking from her face to the gun, he paused, and although he gave nothing away, she could tell that he was thinking fast. Cold, mean, and selfish, Garrett was also scarily intelligent. She was betting that he'd wait for his opportunity to find and destroy both camera and photos.

Without that, she had nothing.

"So," he said at last. "What now?"

"I stay," she said, "and you leave Tammy alone. *Well* alone. In the house, to and from school, and *at* school." Without dropping her gaze from Garrett, she reached across and stroked Tammy's arm soothingly. "Tammy now knows that I know what's been going on. She knows I have evidence. So, no more secrets. She'll tell me if you even *look* at her sideways."

Garrett stared at her steadily. "And in return?"

"In return," she said, "I don't show these photos to either your father or the ladies from the church. What would it do to your reputation, Garrett? Golden Boy Dyson, bullying his little sister? Causing her actual bodily harm?"

"I don't *really* hurt her."

"That's not what it looks like on these photos," she said. "I'm actually not a bad photographer, Garrett. It must be all those years of looking at the effects of wind and light and shade when I'm shooting. I don't miss much." She stared him down. "Either with a camera *or* a gun."

At her words, she saw pure hatred in Garrett's eyes. Nat almost flinched and then reminded herself of what it must have been like for Tammy.

Years of this.

Abruptly, Garrett laughed. He shot a look at Kyle, encouraging him to join in. "All right. Mom hasn't got much longer anyway, and you'll be gone."

"I'll still have the photos," she reminded him. "And I'll still be checking on Tammy. At the first sign of mistreatment, I'll be making those photos public."

Garrett smirked, and Nat knew he was thinking of all the ways he could torment Tammy after she'd gone while ensuring her silence. "Sure," he said. "I've got more to do with my life than waste it on my sister. You've got a deal."

Nat switched her gaze to Kyle. "Kyle?"

He shrugged. "Whatever."

"No," she said. "Not 'whatever'. Do we have a deal?"

"Just say yes," Garrett snapped, glaring at his brother.

"Yes, then!" He cast a disgusted glance at all three of them and stomped off.

Garrett watched him and then looked at Tammy. "Looks like you've got yourself a bodyguard." He grinned without humor. "For now."

"Forever," Nat said, tapping her gun. "Remember that, Garrett. Remember it well."

With one last scathing look at Nat, Garrett slung his backpack over one shoulder and set off after Kyle.

Nat turned to Tammy to find that tears were sliding down her cheeks.

"Oh, hon." She gathered her close and rocked her. "I'm sorry. I'm so sorry you've had to endure that. It's been going on for years, hasn't it?"

She felt Tammy's nod, and the dam broke. The girl cried as though her heart would break. Nat knew that it wasn't only about her bullying brothers or even about her mother, so soon to leave her.

Tammy's whole world was dark. No promise of relief, no love, no future.

Well, she would see about that.

"It'll be all right," Nat said, rocking her. "It will. Really it will. Remember what your mother said when you sang *Que Sera Sera?* That life would bring you all good things and that you should keep looking forward."

Tammy hiccupped. "They'll start again. He said they won't, but they will as soon as you leave. He'll think of a way to get what he wants."

"I know what he has in mind," Nat said. "I've got your brother's measure. But he has no idea of what *I* can do." She eased the girl back from her shoulder and smiled down into those tear-drenched eyes. "I allowed them to think I'm going to walk away, but I'm not. You think I would let my sister go and not protect her little girl?"

"They won't let you stay."

"Oh, I'm not staying," Nat said. "I'll be out the door as fast as I can. But I won't be alone for long." She hugged the girl again. "You'll be coming to live with me, sweetie. I'll do whatever it takes."

Tammy froze. The incredulous hope in her eyes

almost brought her aunt undone. "You'll take me with you? But—but he won't *let* you."

"Let me worry about that. I promise," Nat said. "Whatever it takes. You and me together, that's your future. *I promise.*"

12

Strategy

Natalie Arnold had never been a snoop or a gossip. "Live and let live," had been her approach to life. At times that had been a hard rule hard to adhere to, given that some of the people she'd encountered at the rifle range were rednecks or criminals. Nat simply kept her focus: she was there for the competition. She didn't bad-mouth others, and she didn't join in petitions or lobby groups or demonstrations.

That had worked well up to date, but to get Tammy out of the clutches of her father and brothers, she would have to do something drastic.

The day after she had confronted Garrett and Kyle, she had a window of opportunity. It was Saturday, and Danny had left for a couple of hours on "urgent church business". Garrett was playing football, and Kyle was, as usual, over at his Uncle Rocky's place.

The moment Susannah's eyes drifted shut, Nat beckoned to Tammy and led the way into the kitchen, where she made hot chocolate for Tammy and coffee for herself.

Hot drinks for comfort.

"Right," she said firmly, stirring in sweetener. "Let's talk tactics. What I have seen Garrett do this week is beyond disgraceful." Her eyes flicked up to Tammy's. "In my opinion, the boy is dangerous."

Tammy took a sip of her hot chocolate and said nothing.

Nat frowned. "Has he said anything to you after yesterday's little episode? Threatened you in any way?"

"No." Tammy's lower lip trembled. "He just looks daggers at me." She managed a shaky laugh. "And once, he pointed his finger at me like a gun. No surprise. He hates me."

"Have you always believed that?"

"He and Kyle have never liked me," Tammy said matter-of-factly. "But he's getting worse. And..." she looked away, but not before Nat saw the lost look in her eyes. "Dad doesn't like me, either. He pretends that he treats all of his children the same, but he doesn't."

"No," Nat said, "I've been able to see that for myself. Garrett can do no wrong. He tolerates Kyle. But you?" She shook her head sadly. "I'm not going to pretend, Tammy. I've seen the resentment in his eyes, once or twice when he didn't know I was watching him."

"I don't know why. I try to be good." Tammy leaned her chin on her hand and stared at her aunt. "He never liked me saying anything about Garrett, and he hates it when I cry. It just makes him madder... but when I was little, I couldn't help it." She hesitated. "I cried when he told us Mom was going to die, and even then, he was angry."

Nat stared at her. "What did he say?"

"He told me if I kept crying, he wouldn't let me sit with her."

Nat swore and then immediately apologized. "Pardon me, Tammy. That man is a monster. He and Garrett make a good pair."

Tammy managed a watery smile. "You're the only one who has ever believed me."

Nat reached across and took her hand. "Didn't you tell your mother?"

"I tried when I was little, but Garrett always acted innocent and made it sound like I was telling lies." She shrugged wearily. "Mom believed him almost every time. And Dad used to get angry."

"And no doubt the more your brother got away with, the worse he got." At Tammy's nod, she asked, "What about Kyle?"

"He's mean too, but in a different way. He used to hurt me more when we were little, but Garrett's meaner." She thought about that for a moment, then added, "Kyle's not clever enough to say the kind of things that Garrett does, so he does what Garrett says instead."

"OK." Nat drank more coffee and then said, "It sounds to me that you've been emotionally abused for years by the males in this family, with a bit of rough handling thrown in. I'm concerned that Garrett's bad behavior is escalating, and the physical abuse is becoming more serious. Would you agree?"

Tammy nodded, drooping.

"Your mother has never intervened? Never noticed anything?"

"She did once, when Dad made me bend over the fence and hit me with his belt," Tammy said, looking ashamed at the memory of her humiliation. "He says it's a case of "spare the rod and spoil the child" but Mom was furious. She made him promise never to do it again, but he said she had to let him discipline the boys the way he wanted to."

"Another reason for them to hate you," Nat said gently. "They got beaten; you didn't."

"Except that he's never had to beat Garrett like that," Tammy said. "Because he's always *good*. Or he pretends to be."

"What did you do for him to beat you?"

"He said I lied."

"About?"

"About Garrett pushing me out of a tree."

At her aunt's arched eyebrow and spread hands, she added, "Garrett said he didn't, and he told this long story...." She hesitated and then shook her head. "I can't even tell it to you because it *sounds* as though I'm lying. He twisted some things that happened, and it sounded like I was making up a whole bunch of lies. And then Garrett put on this big show of making excuses for me and asking Dad to ignore it. He said *he* had already forgiven me. That made Dad madder because Garrett was showing Christian charity, and I was still denying it all... you see?"

"I do. Unfortunately."

"Don't blame Mom," Tammy said pleadingly. "When I was little, it sounded like I was a tattle-tale. And Garrett knew how to make it seem like I was just looking for sympathy while he was the one getting hurt. Then he got better at it, and Mom would get upset because she'd be caught between me and Dad and the boys. And now she's sick, so we *can't* worry her."

Nat got up, moved beside Tammy, and wrapped her

arms around the girl. "We won't. I love my sister, Tammy, never doubt that. She's got a beautiful soul, but she's totally trusting, which can be a weakness. And she's never been able to deal with conflict."

At Tammy's nod, she went on, "Susannah has a blind spot when it comes to the handsome, plausible men in her family. First your father, now Garrett. You're the one paying for that." Giving her niece one final kiss on the head, she took her seat again. "The problem is that your mother is the one thing that stood between you and them."

"I know." Tammy gulped her hot chocolate and then took a deep breath. "Did you really mean it when you said I could go with you?"

"A promise is a promise." Nat sent her a twisted smile. "But I can't just sue for custody. Your father would win, without a doubt. He's respected in the community; he's a law-abiding citizen and a devout member of the church. As for Garrett, he's the local hero."

"Then how?" Still raw from everything that had been happening to her, Tammy looked beaten. "What can you do?"

Nat drummed her fingers on the table while she regarded her niece. "The apple doesn't fall far from the tree, I'm thinking, when it comes to Garrett and his father. Garrett has plenty to hide, and I'm guessing that Danny Dyson has too. After a few things the church women let drop, I've been watching him, and I'm curious. When did he start up that Retreat on the land your uncle rents to him, out at the farm?"

Tammy shook her head. "I'm not sure. Years ago?"

"It sounds like he makes a reasonable living from that, but he makes sizable donations to the church, so

I've heard," Nat said. "The church ladies are under the impression that he supports overseas missions, as well as helping out people locally. But for him to be able to maintain a family, plus make those donations... it doesn't add up."

"He's frugal. That's what he says. He doesn't like to spend money."

"Not on you, maybe," Nat said. "And what's the connection between him and your Uncle Rocky?"

"They're brothers." Tammy looked confused.

"I know that. Your father is over there at the Retreat almost every day, as far as I can ascertain, but why is Kyle there?"

Tammy shook her head. "I don't know. He helps out around the farm."

"Yet the farm doesn't produce." Nat frowned. "From what I hear, your Uncle Rocky walks a fine line with the law."

"He's been in trouble, but Dad says he can be saved."

"Convenient," Nat said. "What do you think? Does that sound like the kind of relationship your father has with your uncle? Trying to convert him to the right path?"

The girl's brow furrowed while she thought about it. "He counsels people in the church. They come to his office. But I've never heard him say anything about Rocky. Except once he warned Kyle that he'd better not *ever* find him getting into trouble with the law." She made a face. "And then he yelled at me because he knew that I'd heard what he said."

Nat nodded, her mind working. "All right. Well, here's what I'm going to do. The only way I can take you home to live with me is if I have something to hold over your father's head. Something he doesn't want people to know. And now that I'm getting a clearer picture of him and Garrett—and Kyle, I suppose—I'm willing to bet there's something to find. So my job is to find it." She leaned forward and held Tammy's gaze. "All you have to do is to stay out of the way. Keep things calm. Don't stir up your brothers or your father. Let them think that they can do what they like once I'm gone, and don't act too friendly towards me."

"OK." There was a faint light of hope in Tammy's eyes. "Can I help? Try to listen in when he's speaking to Garrett and Kyle?" Then she bit her lip. "That won't be easy. He usually takes them into his office and shuts the door."

"No. Absolutely not. I don't want to give them any reason to suspect either of us, and *you* need to stay safe. Be careful, Tammy." She smiled gently. "Just focus on your mother."

That made them both think of how little time they had left with her, and Tammy looked away, her eyes damp.

"Go in and sit with her now," Nat said. "But sit near the window, and tell me if you see your father's car coming up the driveway."

"What are you going to do?" Tammy's eyes widened.

"I'm going to snoop," Nat said. "Starting with his office. And I'm going to be doing it every chance I get."

13

Locked Doors

NAT COULDN'T HELP a nervous glance over her shoulder as she stepped over the threshold of her brother-in-law's office, even though she knew that Tammy and Susannah were the only other two in the house. Prying into other people's business felt totally alien.

Tammy, she reminded herself. It was all about Tammy.

She closed the door behind her and just stood there for a moment, staring around. Danny hadn't stinted on his home office. The room was larger than the sitting room, and tastefully furnished in soothing tones of blue and cream, with warmth added by polished redwood furniture. Two comfortable easy chairs and a small sofa were grouped around a coffee table near the window, and just behind them on a low credenza was a sound system and racks of CDs.

Comfortable seating for two people or a small group. Danny's counseling sessions, no doubt.

And somewhere he could bring people when he wanted privacy to discuss his business.

Everything was spotlessly clean. The desk was large and clear of clutter, except for a computer monitor and a keyboard. Several cables led down to the tower containing the hard drives and a LaserJet printer/copier on a small table next to the desk. Against the wall stood a filing cabinet, next to a cupboard with glass-fronted doors on the top half. The wall on one end was nothing but bookshelves, filled with books, folders, and file boxes.

It all looked very organized and innocent, but he was hiding something in here. She knew it.

The desk, she thought. She would start there, work her way around the room. Nat walked around behind the desk and started with the drawer on the left. It slid out easily, but there was nothing to see but a clear perspex organizer neatly filled with pens, pencils, rulers, and paper clips. She pulled the drawer out as far as it would go and lifted out the organizer to peer under it, bending down low enough to check that nothing was stuck at the back.

Nothing. She closed the drawer and was about to move to the one underneath it when she spotted the thumbprint she'd left on the shiny drawer pull.

Her heart gave a thump. With the obsession with cleanliness that Danny Dyson had demonstrated in this room, it was entirely possible he'd notice something like that. She cleaned the thumbprint off with the hem of her t-shirt and stood there, thinking.

Don't rush it.

She needed to make sure that everything she touched was put back just as she found it. Depending on what he was up to—and whether he expected her to pry —he might or might not be setting traps for anyone poking around.

She was sunk if he was the type to conceal hairs or something else that would easily dislodge. There was no way she could anticipate that. But surely he wasn't that paranoid?

Get a grip, she told herself. She'd been here several weeks and hadn't set foot in his office. It wasn't likely that she would start nosing around now, when Susannah was getting sicker by the day. Danny should be feeling reasonably secure.

To hell with it. If he realized she'd been in his office and confronted her, she'd deal with it then.

Then a thought struck her, and she went to her room to get her camera. If she took a photo of the drawers and the cupboards before moving things, she could make sure she put everything back the right way.

For the next forty minutes, she went through all the drawers and cupboards, checking and re-checking that nothing was out of place as she finished each one. The four-drawer filing cabinet was locked. Frustrated, she did a quick search for a concealed key, but Danny either kept the key with him or had hidden it too well.

Natalie stood in front of it, arms folded. *That's* where the proof she needed was: right there.

The filing cabinet *could* contain notes on private counseling sessions, but somehow she doubted it. In the two weeks she'd been here, Danny had ushered people into his office just twice. The first time it had been a woman, accompanied by a teenage daughter. She looked upset and furious, while the girl's face looked mutinous. They came out looking calmer. Danny had his arm loosely around the woman's shoulder, radiating compassion and comfort.

The second time it was just one man, tall and distinguished with a grave face. He nodded politely at Nat, saying, "Pleased to meet you, Ma'am. A sad time, I'm afraid," when Danny introduced her as his sister-in-law.

He had not bothered to tell Nat who his visitor was, but she thought she heard Danny call him Lawrence.

Well, maybe details of those two visits were in the filing cabinet; maybe they weren't. But in four large drawers, surely she'd find *something* that Danny wanted to keep hidden.

Blackmail. She forced herself to say the word, stark on her lips. That was what she was looking at, pure and simple. Something she could use to blackmail Danny Dyson so he'd let his daughter go.

It would have to be something big.

Glancing at her watch, she saw that Danny had been gone almost an hour and a half.

Time to get out of here, tend to Susannah, and think about where that key might be.

$$—————————————————$$

14

Promises

$$—————————————————$$

WHILE HER AUNT Nat was searching her father's office, Tammy sat quietly in the chair by her mother's bedside, keeping a wary eye on the driveway while she darned a pair of her father's socks that were wearing thin on the heel.

It made no sense to darn socks when they were so cheap to buy, and she didn't think they weren't *that* short of money. But frugality was one of her father's hobby horses. "A penny saved is a penny earned" was one of his favorite sayings. There were others, too, and Tammy had heard them all so many times she switched off when he started lecturing about minimalism and watching the pennies. He insisted that she wear her clothes until they wore out, as long as they still fit her. The past year she had filled out so much that he had no choice but to let her re-stock her wardrobe, but half of her clothes came from the charity bags that the church ladies sorted through.

Garrett and Kyle's wardrobe was also subject to scrutiny, but somehow Garrett managed to engineer 'donations' of brand-name clothes that looked suspiciously pristine. Tammy noticed, though, that he took care to wear older clothes around the house in the evening and at weekends to appease his father.

Kyle didn't care. He customarily threw on the first thing at hand and was more likely to be in trouble for skipping a shower or looking scruffy.

Inspecting her handiwork, Tammy decided that it was good enough to earn her a grunt from her father instead of a command to re-do it. She put the socks aside and turned her attention to her mother. Right now, she looked peaceful, with the frown lines on her forehead smoothed out and her blonde hair spread out on the pillow. Her cheekbones were more prominent, and her arm, resting on the sheet, looked thin and frail. Her hand was partly open, her fingers curled loosely, and Tammy couldn't help putting out a hand and linking her fingers with her mother's.

"I'm going to miss you, Mom," she whispered.

Her mind turned to the fun times, the hours when they'd snuggle up under a rug to watch a classic movie, singing along with the songs. That's how Tammy had learned to sing. Over and over and over, singing along with her mother until their voices had become one, and she knew all the old songs off by heart.

Her voice had always been pure and sweet, and she had joined the children's choir at the church the moment her father gave permission. It wasn't long before she was performing solos, as well as duets with her mother and a few others.

Her father never minded the hours the two of them put in at the church. His wife thought he was being generous, but Tammy knew instinctively that he gave permission because it reflected well on him, having his beautiful wife and angelic little girl there in front of everyone.

And Garrett, of course, attended Sunday school and services and charmed everyone he met, even before he started to become a star on the football field.

Her mother's fingers turned and squeezed Tammy's, and when Tammy looked at her, her eyes were open and shining with love.

"I'm going to miss you too, baby girl," she said. "That's one of the worst things about having to leave this earth so soon." She stroked Tammy's fingers with her thumb. "If it's my time, it's my time, but I'm going to miss you all so much. Darling Danny, and my sweet Garrett, and blunt old Kyle. And my talented, gorgeous girl."

Tammy's throat seized up, so she couldn't speak. How was she going to bear it?

"Look after them for me, Tammy, won't you?" She smiled gently. "I know you don't have to be asked; you're such a good little thing. But Garrett will be going off to college soon, and Kyle is such… a *boy*. Your father will need you."

Tammy closed her eyes, conflicted. What could she say? She couldn't lie to her mother. Not on her *deathbed*. But she couldn't promise to stay; she *couldn't*.

Despite her efforts to choke back the tears, she let out a convulsive sob.

"*Que sera, sera*, baby," her mother said softly. "What will be, will be."

Tammy swallowed. That, she could deal with.

"I'll remember, Mom," she finally managed. "What will be, will be. I promise you that I'll do whatever needs to be done, as far as Dad and Garrett and Kyle are concerned."

That wasn't precisely what her mother had asked, but it seemed to satisfy her.

"Thank you, sweetie. And look after yourself."

"I will." Tammy blinked hard until her vision was clear again. "Aunt Nat says she'll look out for me."

"That's wonderful. She's been so good to us. We had our differences as children, and I'll never understand this thing she has with guns, but she's a good soul. I'm glad she'll be staying in touch." Her mother's eyes closed again. "I'm tired today. I might doze a little, but can you stay? For just a little while?"

"Of course."

"And sing," her mother murmured. "Our song, baby. Sing our song."

So Tammy did. But even while her eyes were on her mother's face, her mind was with her aunt.

Please find something. Please.

15

Another Confrontation

WHEN DANNY CAME BACK from offering solace and suggestions to Maeve McCray and her scared, pregnant fifteen-year-old daughter Jenna, his sister-in-law was busy in the kitchen. He paused at the doorway, struck anew by how different Susannah and her sister were. Natalie was tall and verging on skinny; flat-chested in a plain white cotton sleeveless shirt and knee-length denim shorts. Her chestnut hair was cropped short, and cool gray eyes looked out of a face that was all angles. Natalie's genes, he knew, were all from her father's side of the family.

Thank God Susannah had taken after her mother.

Sensing his eyes on her, Natalie glanced at him with her usual impassive expression. "Lunch won't be too much longer. I'm assuming it'll be just you, me, and Tammy?"

"That's right." Just to be ornery, he treated her to the full-wattage Danny Dyson smile, the one had most of the parishioners eating out of his hand. "Let me say again how much I appreciate all you do for us, Natalie."

"No trouble at all," she said without looking at him, assembling a sandwich.

In a good mood from the effusive gratitude heaped upon him for his counsel, Danny eyed her narrowly. He'd *make* her talk to him.

"May I ask you something, Natalie?"

"Sure." She didn't look up.

"What's your opinion of Susannah's condition?"

Startled into making eye contact, she stopped and stared at him. "Why? Has the doctor said something?"

"No, no." He moved across the room and rested his hand on her arm, knowing she'd hate it. "I know what *she* says. I want to know what you think."

She edged away, and smiling inwardly; he removed his hand.

"Susannah is clearly declining," she said.

He nodded. "That much is obvious. But her general mood?"

Natalie regarded him warily. "Acceptance. Sadness, of course, at…." She hesitated before going on, "At the prospect of having to leave you all. As for her pain, I think it's being controlled pretty well."

"She seems very tired."

"I think she is, yes. But that's to be expected, from what the doctor says."

"You don't think that Tammy is spending too much time with her? That her visits should be limited somewhat, so as not to tire Susannah?"

He saw her shoulders tense, and as she straightened up, the flash of dislike in her eyes was unmistakable. "No, Danny, I don't. Much of the time, they don't even talk. Tammy just sits with her or sings when Susannah asks her to. It seems to comfort her, having Tammy there."

He nodded. "Well, we'll monitor it on a day-to-day basis, then. And what about you? How are *you* holding up?" He touched her arm again.

"I'm fine." This time she didn't move away, but the tension between them vibrated.

"You're not finding it all too much? Or worrying about losing your competitive edge?" He smiled. "Are you getting in enough practice out the back on those targets you set up?"

"Enough to keep my hand in. And no, it's not all too much. Excuse me." Natalie stepped around him and reached up to get four plates from the cupboard. "It's a privilege to be able to look after my sister in her last days."

"Well, six weeks at the most, and you'll be able to return to your life. And we'll have to find a way to move on with ours." Unexpectedly, the stark reality of Susannah's departure hit him all over again when he uttered the words 'six weeks', and his voice cracked.

Annoyed with himself, he turned to look out of the window. He'd intended to rub it in that Natalie would not be part of Tammy's life after Susannah's death; he hadn't meant to show weakness.

For a moment, she said nothing, which gave him a chance to regroup. Then he heard her voice, a little hesitant. "What *are* your plans, Danny? How will you cope with the boys and a daughter barely into her teens?"

Back in control, he turned to face her. Always sensitive to the moods of others, he instantly understood that this was what she really wanted to know.

Tammy.

"We have a very supportive church community, as you know. They'll help. Luckily, the children don't need babysitters any longer. Also…." he shrugged. "Tammy is old enough to step up and take up the reins in the house."

"She's still at school, Danny. Just a child." Natalie's voice was even, but her gaze held a hint of steel.

"God never gives us a load greater than we can carry," he told her. "Try not to look at this from a modern perspective, Natalie. In years gone by, Tammy would be getting close to marriageable age. And she doesn't need school. There will be plenty for her to do, helping me to minister to the needs of the parish, taking on Susannah's role running the house."

"You're not taking her out of school!" Natalie looked horrified.

"Of course not." He allowed himself to sound a little testy. "She'll stay there until she's legally allowed to leave. Until then, we'll manage."

"But what about what Tammy wants from life? Doesn't she get a say?"

"When she's twenty-one, she can decide. Until then, she will do the right thing." He folded his arms. "Tammy has had a very easy life until now. You haven't really been part of our lives, so you wouldn't be aware of it, but I'm afraid the child has been spoiled. Regrettably, Tammy has been Susannah's blind spot."

Natalie finally cracked, and she glared at him. "So all Tammy can look forward is a life of menial work and strict discipline, is that what you're saying?"

"Not at all," he said, sending her a reproachful look. "A life characterized by service to others, perhaps, but there's nothing wrong with that, Natalie. She'll still have the church choir. She enjoys that."

He saw a muscle twitch in her cheek.

"And where do I fit into this? Do I still get to see her?"

"I'm sure you'll want to visit the children now and then. But it might be a good idea to phone first, in case it's a busy time."

He could see that she had received the message loud and clear: there was no place for Natalie Arnold in Tammy's life.

She stared at him for a few long seconds and then said abruptly, "Lunch is ready whenever you are. I'll prepare a plate for Susannah, but I doubt she'll eat much."

"Thank you. I'll just go and say hello to my wife and send Tammy out."

Satisfied with the exchange, he nodded at her pleasantly and left the room.

16

A Visit to the Doctor

EIGHT FRUSTRATING DAYS went by before Nat finally had a breakthrough. She searched every place she could think of that might conceal the key to the filing cabinet, without luck. It wasn't taped to the back of the filing cabinet, under the rug, in a vase, or tucked away above the curtains.

She also spent more time chatting with Marie and Grace and others who visited. From the snippets she gleaned, Danny Dyson didn't appear to have a huge income, after paying a small staff out at the Retreat and making his donations.

That didn't fit with the real Danny Dyson. There *was* something there, she was certain. He had a legion of fans, but there had been one female visitor who couldn't hide the cynical curl to her lip when Susannah talked about Danny. When the woman saw Nat's speculative look, her face smoothed out, and she turned away. So, not everyone was taken in by him.

Time was passing, and Susannah was clearly deterio-rating. What if she didn't have weeks? What if her sister took a turn for the worse, and she had nothing to bargain with?

There was no way on God's earth that she was leaving Tammy behind.

She was considering a stealthy expedition to Rocky's farm to see if that offered any clues when she finally saw the key.

She tapped on the office door to let Danny know supper was ready. He was bending over, slipping some papers into a folder in the bottom drawer, and the key was still in the lock in the top right-hand corner. Unfortunately, it was attached to a fob that held Danny's main set of keys: the house, the car, the church.

Annoyed with herself, she cursed silently. All that time wasted searching the room, the kitchen, the living room—and it had been on his keyring the whole time.

At the sound of her knock, Danny slid the drawer closed and stood upright. He locked the cabinet and dropped the keys into his pocket as he turned, one eyebrow raised.

"Supper's ready," she said. "Five minutes?"

"Thank you, Natalie." He moved to his desk, now clear of papers, and shut down his computer. "I wonder… if you're doing a run to town tomorrow, could you drop my suit off at the dry cleaner?"

A power play, she knew. The church women usually did that kind of thing for him, but he knew the next day was shopping day, and he liked to give Nat extra little tasks.

"Just leave it out for me. I'll take it in." She walked away, thinking furiously.

She had to get that key.

Or *access* to the key.

Could she somehow make a copy of it?

She almost groaned. She wasn't some kind of super-spy, nor did she know anyone who might know how to do that kind of thing. Didn't people make an impression of a key in clay or something?

Like *that* was something she had just conveniently lying around. And even if she did, what then? She couldn't imagine any reputable locksmith making a key from a clay impression.

Think, Nat, think.

She turned her attention back to Danny's key fob. It was usually in his pocket; he never hung his keys up on the key rack near the door. If he changed clothes to go out—to a funeral, to a meeting, whatever—he'd simply switch keys from one pocket to another. When he sat down to watch TV, he still kept them with him.

Think.

He'd have to take his keys out of his pocket to take a shower, and he'd have to put them somewhere while he slept.

The more her mind turned over the possibilities, the more downhearted she felt. This was not going to be easy.

How? *How?*

After breakfast the next day, Nat called to schedule an appointment with her sister's GP, a pleasant middle-aged woman who had seen Susannah through all of her pregnancies and was monitoring her through her last days. Dr. Morris's schedule was full for the next two days, but when the receptionist, Corinne, realized who it was, she said immediately, "Just come anyway. I'll fit you in. How's Susannah doing?"

Nat sighed, not really knowing how to answer. "Oh well… you know. She's always cheerful, but…."

"Yes, I know." Julia's voice was sympathetic. "She's a wonderful lady. Everyone loves Susannah. Well, we'll see you later, OK?"

At the surgery, she filled in forms and waited for twenty minutes before Dr. Morris ushered another patient out and beckoned to Nat. When the door closed behind them, Nat said, "Thanks for seeing me at such short notice."

Dr. Morris looked at her keenly. "Are you here for yourself, or is this about Susannah?"

"For myself," Nat said. "I know you're already doing everything you can for my sister."

"Her meds are doing the job?"

"They seem to be."

"She'll need to increase the morphine soon," Dr. Morris said gently. "Since she refuses to come into the palliative care unit…."

"There's no chance of that," Nat said. "She wants to be at home when she…goes."

Why was it so hard to say *when she dies*?

"Many people prefer to be in their own homes, in their own bed. And you still have plenty of help from the church group?"

"Yes, they're wonderful," Nat said sincerely. "We're all so grateful to them." She smiled wryly. "I've never eaten so much cake."

Dr. Morris laughed. "I can imagine. So, Natalie, what can I do for you?"

Natalie steeled herself. It wasn't really a lie; she *was* having trouble sleeping.

"I could do with something to help me sleep," she said. "I tend to lie awake, worrying about Susannah and the kids, and when I do sleep, I just doze. I'm awake at the tiniest sound, even if it's just one of the kids using the bathroom or Danny making coffee."

The other woman nodded. She was aware that Danny had now moved a big, comfortable recliner into the bedroom and slept there most of the night, tending to Susannah whenever she needed anything. "He's up and down all night, I imagine."

"He won't let anyone else do it. I've offered, but..." she shrugged. "I see her all day, while Danny's out and about with church work...and his own work, I guess. He wants her to himself at night."

"Understandable." Dr. Morris's face softened. "They're very close. A lovely family. I'm so sorry."

"Thanks," Nat said, forcing a smile. "I guess you see this sort of thing all too often."

"I do, yes."

The doctor picked up a pen and pulled the prescription pad towards her. "Any allergies?"

"No."

She started scribbling. "These are generally pretty effective, with minimal side effects. Start with just one, and increase the dosage as needed; the instructions will be on the label." She flicked a glance at Nat. "No driving after taking them because naturally, they'll make you drowsy."

"How many can I safely take?" Nat asked. "Just in case...after the funeral, I..." she shook her head. "This is hard."

"I wouldn't recommend any more than three; if you have serious problems with sleeping after a few months go by, go and see your doctor back home." Dr. Morris tore the page off the pad and handed it to her. "Will you be staying on for a while to take care of the children?"

"Probably not for long," Nat said, her heart beating erratically at the thought. "I think their father wants to establish a set routine as quickly as possible. And he has a lot of willing helpers."

Dr. Morris nodded. "Anything else I can help you with?"

"No," Nat said, folding the prescription and putting it in her pocket. "That's it for now. Thank you."

She would go to the drugstore and have it filled immediately.

If three pills would be enough to knock her out, then she'd use four in Danny Dyson's coffee.

Or maybe even five.

17

Harsh Words

THE DRUGSTORE WAS BUSY, and Nat had to wait in a queue for her prescription to be filled. She picked up some multivitamins as well and was reaching for shampoo when a voice sounded at her elbow. "Natalie?"

She turned to find snowy-haired Marie Kelly from the church smiling at her.

"Oh, hi, Marie."

"How's Susannah today? She seemed a bit down when I left yesterday."

"Not too bad," Nat said, summoning up a smile in return. Marie was a good-hearted soul who genuinely cared for Susannah. "Every day has its ups and downs."

"You know you can call on me any time you need a break, don't you?"

"Yes, I know. So far, we're doing okay. But thanks."

"All right." Marie gave her a quick hug. "I'm so glad you're staying. Susannah needed her sister, I think. Anyway, I have to run; I just wanted to say hello. I'll see you in a couple of days." With a flutter of her fingers, she left.

Nat watched her go and then bent to pluck the shampoo off the shelf. As she did, another voice said, "Excuse me."

Nat straightened and found herself looking at a woman in her fifties. Her dark hair showed a line of grey at the part, and her face was lined and tired.

And determined.

Nat felt a curl of unease. "Yes?"

"I couldn't help overhearing what Marie was saying. Are you Susannah Dyson's sister?"

"Yes, that's right."

The woman hesitated. "She has cancer, I believe."

"Yes, she has." Nat was becoming more and more uncomfortable. "I'm Natalie. Nat. And you…?"

"I'm Loretta Paxton," she said, her eyes drilling into Nat's. She waited as though her name should mean something.

"I'm sorry, Susannah hasn't mentioned you." Nat waited.

"No," Loretta said. "I imagine she wouldn't." A muscle jumped in her jaw.

Uh oh, thought Nat. She gestured towards the counter. "Well, uh, my prescription should be just about ready…."

"I almost didn't say anything," the woman went on, "and I wouldn't want to wish cancer on anyone… of course I wouldn't. But you should know, your family has destroyed *my* family. Saint Danny, doing his good deeds, turning my mother's head, so she left almost everything to *him.* My kids needed that money." Her eyes suddenly filled with tears. "You don't know how much they needed it. And you can't tell me that Susannah didn't know; that she didn't want the money. And it's not just us, either. I…" she stopped and shook her head.

Stunned, Nat just stared at her, clutching the multivitamins and shampoo, and then finally found her voice. "Susannah wouldn't…."

"Susannah! Always as nice as pie, but she——" the woman choked on the words. "She would never hear a bad word about *him*, but she can't be any better than he is to turn a blind eye like that." She turned on her heel and walked away, throwing over her shoulder, "He'll be seen for what he is one day, but it'll be too late for me. Too late for my kids."

Feeling sick, Nat watched her walk up the aisle and out of the door. When it swung shut behind her, she glanced around to find several curious sets of eyes on her. Putting her chin in the air and keeping her eyes straight ahead, she made her way back to the counter.

If she didn't have plans for those sleeping pills, she would have put everything back on the shelves and walked out. But now, more than ever, she wanted to see what Danny Dyson had in his filing cabinet.

Whatever he was up to, he was dragging her sister's name through the mud too. What had the woman said about her mother? "*She left everything to HIM.*"

Gritting her teeth, she waited impatiently. At least she had a starting point.

18

Evidence

NAT RAN through it in her mind, over and over. Drug Danny. Steal the key. Photocopy anything that looks suspicious. Replace the key.

Her heart was in her mouth at the very thought.

What if she didn't use enough of the pills, and he woke up? What if she used too many and he slept for half the morning? Or didn't wake up at all?

No, she was sure there'd be enough of a safety margin to cater for idiots who might over-medicate.

What if he could taste something funny in the coffee?

What if, what if. *Stop it, Nat. Just do it.*

The next day, when he left the house to do whatever the heck Danny Dyson did all day, she wrote down the model of his LaserJet printer. She couldn't take it for granted that there would be enough toner left for the job, so she'd buy some more.

Paper, she thought. She'd better buy more paper, too.

A quick trip to town gave her what she needed.

While she was there, she mailed a spare camera card with copies of the damning photos to Molly, with a note asking her to take care of it until she got back. Although she had hidden her camera in the middle of a pile of t-shirts, and her computer was password-protected, she didn't trust Garrett further than she could kick him.

Now, whatever he did, the photos were safe.

She decided to try the sleeping pills out on herself first. Danny liked his coffee with plenty of cream and sugar. She didn't know whether that was a good or a bad thing; if it were black and strong, would that mask the taste of the pills better? Or would the sugar disguise the taste?

Movies made all of this look so easy. Real life was different.

As usual, she made Danny a cup of coffee before she went to bed and tapped lightly on the bedroom door.

He was sitting in the recliner with his feet up, reading a book. Susannah was fast asleep. These days, she spent a lot of time sleeping.

"A treat for you," she said, handing him the mug and a plate with a generous slice of carrot cake topped with white frosting. "Marie brought this today. She said it's your favorite."

He nodded, treating her to his polite-Danny smile. "Indeed it is. The ladies are spoiling me."

Nat watched him scoop up a blob of frosting from the plate and lick it off his finger. That sweet tooth might come in handy. Perhaps she could put some of the sleeping pills in the cake frosting and some in the coffee?

She glanced at Susannah. "Has she been sleeping since supper?"

He followed her gaze to the still form of his wife,

and his mouth turned down. "Yes. It takes very little to tire her these days."

Nat nodded, feeling the usual heavy weight in her chest when she looked at her sister. "Well, I'm off to bed. Good night."

"Good night." With another token smile, he went back to his book, sipping his coffee.

Nat returned to the kitchen and stared at the two coffee mugs in front of her.

One was a duplicate of what she had just given Danny.

The other was identical except for the addition of four crushed sleeping pills.

Nat tasted the first one and made a face. Ugh. Way too sweet for her.

She tasted the second one, frowning in concentration.

They tasted the same to her.

She took another tentative sip of the one with crushed pills.

Nothing. Okay, that was how she would proceed, then.

She poured the contents of both mugs down the sink and took two pills with a drink of water. She didn't dare take four, not when she'd never taken a sleeping pill in her life. Two might give her some idea of the effect of four.

Nat switched off the kitchen light and went to bed, moving quietly, so she didn't wake Tammy. The girl's nights were restless enough as it was.

The next morning, she didn't hear Tammy get up. In fact, she didn't wake until Tammy shook her and whispered, "Aunt Nat?"

She grunted and forced one eye open. It was like lifting weights. "Tammy…?" she said drowsily, and then thought, *Susannah…*

Feeling as though her head was stuffed with cotton wool, she struggled upright. "Tams…your Mom…is she—"

"Mom's fine," she said. "I made breakfast, but I have to go to school. Are *you* okay?"

The sleeping pills, Nat remembered. She pushed aside the cotton bedspread. "Tams, I'm so sorry. I can't believe I overslept. Why didn't you wake me sooner?"

"Dad said not to. He said you probably needed it."

Wanting nothing more than to slide back under the sheets and close her eyes again, Nat groaned. "I'm sorry, sweetie." She focused on Tammy and frowned. The girl was upset but trying to hide it.

"You made breakfast?" Nat said. "For your father and brothers?"

Tammy nodded and avoided her eyes. She shouldered her backpack. "I have to go. The bus will be here soon."

"They gave you a hard time, didn't they?" *Darn it,* Nat thought. She had made a point of being at every meal, determined not to give the Dyson males a chance to pick on Tammy.

Tammy shrugged, still not looking at her. "It's okay. See you this afternoon, Aunt Nat."

One time, she thought bitterly. She'd dropped the ball just once since the day she'd confronted Garrett and

Kyle, and they had immediately seized the opportunity to make Tammy miserable again.

Listening to Tammy's soft farewell to her mother and then to the sound of the front door closing, Nat forced herself out of bed.

Right. Tonight, then. She'd find what she needed to get Tammy away from here.

19

Dinner

THAT AFTERNOON, when they arrived home, both Garrett and Kyle smiled at her, which immediately made her grit her teeth. Kyle preferred dark looks to smiles, and this one was more of a smirk, which told her that he felt he had put one over her at breakfast, seizing the opportunity to get in a few digs at Tammy. Garrett was excessively polite, putting himself out to be charming.

His way of showing that he was the top dog.

Nat decided to pretend that she knew nothing. Instead, she cooked roast pork with the crackliest crackling she could manage. Home-made apple sauce, crisp roast potatoes, and Danny's favorite for dessert: blueberry pie with a crust to die for and rich vanilla bean ice cream.

"Wow," Garrett said, sitting back and patting his stomach, and pushing his plate away. "Super meal, Aunt Nat."

"To make up for sleeping in this morning," she said, smiling around at them all. "Sorry about that. I guess it all caught up with me." She raised an eyebrow at Danny. "Seconds?"

"You'll make me fat," he said jovially, but she didn't miss the wariness in his eyes. "Yes, thank you."

She was being *too* friendly. She'd better tone it down.

"Nothing wrong with good food," she said. "And plenty of it."

"You might teach my daughter a few of your skills before you leave," he said, accepting the plate from her when she returned with his second helping. "I know she tries, and we appreciate her efforts, but she has some way to go. As we told her this morning." He sampled a spoonful of pie. "Now this, Tammy, is what I'm talking about. It's a pity your mother didn't pass on her secrets before…well." He cut himself off and kept eating.

Tammy looked down at her plate and listlessly dug into the pie with her spoon.

"I'll be happy to stay an extra month or two and teach her to cook," Nat said, keeping her voice pleasant. "Would you like me to do that?"

Danny, Garrett, and Kyle all stopped eating and looked at her. Danny and Garrett maintained a neutral expression. Kyle looked aghast but managed to cover it quickly.

Tammy didn't even look up.

"Thank you," Danny said. "But Marie has already volunteered to give Tammy a few lessons. We've disrupted your life enough."

Nat simply nodded. "Okay. Well, any time you need me, all you have to do is call."

"That's very generous of you." Danny switched his attention to his youngest son. "Garrett, how did you do in that science exam last week? I've been remiss in not asking you."

"A-Plus," Garrett said nonchalantly. "I burned the midnight oil studying for that one. Had to, with football training and the church working bee."

His father nodded his approval. "Nothing worth having comes easily; always remember that." He swallowed more pie and then focused on Kyle. "And you, Kyle? Did you do those jobs for your uncle?"

"Yeah." Catching his father's frown, he amended it hastily. "I mean, yes, I did." He shot a jealous glance at Garrett. "And I helped at the working bee, too."

"Uh-huh." Danny smiled politely at Nat. "This is *excellent* pie. As good as anything Susannah has made, I must admit."

"Thank you."

Silence reigned for a few moments while he and the boys finished dessert.

Danny sat back and looked at Tammy's plate. She had barely touched her dessert. "Eat what's put in front of you, Tammy."

She scooped a tiny amount of ice cream onto her spoon and ate it.

Her father looked at her thoughtfully. "I'm afraid I've lost track of how you're doing at school, Tammy. You had English and History exams recently, I believe."

"Yes." She raised her eyes to his, looking like a puppy waiting to be beaten.

"And…?"

She swallowed. "I got a C."

"In what?"

"In, um, both."

He looked at her expressionlessly. "Cs."

"I'm sorry. It's hard to concentrate at school right now."

"Garrett and Kyle still manage to do what needs to be done." He frowned and nodded at her plate. "Keep eating."

Tammy ate some more ice cream.

"Life is not easy for any of us right now, Tammy. We need to be strong. Do you understand?"

"Yes," she whispered.

"I beg your pardon?"

"Yes, Dad."

"Very well then. I expect an improvement next time. Tough times really show what people are made of." He pushed his chair back. "I'm going to sit with your mother now. You can say goodnight to her, but then I think you should spend a few hours studying."

Garrett had been watching the exchange closely, and now he chose to speak up. "Dad, if I might say something?"

His father raised an eyebrow.

"It's probably harder for Tammy," Garrett said. "She's the youngest, and a girl. Maybe give her a break this time. Let her sit with Mom for half an hour?"

A muscle twitched in Danny Dyson's jaw. He stared at Garrett, who was looking back with clear blue eyes so much like his mother's, and then he glanced at Tammy before standing up.

"That," he said, "is *typical* of your brother. Remember this before you come running to me with tales about him. You may sit with your mother for thirty minutes after you help your aunt with the washing up. But first, finish that food."

He nodded at Nat and left the room, closely followed by a smug Garrett and a sulky Kyle.

Nat put a hand over Tammy's shaking fingers. "Do you want any more?"

Tammy cast a look at the door as though expecting to see her father standing there. "No. Not really. It's delicious, but—"

"I know," Nat said. "Give it to me."

She made short work of the pie and then stood up, pausing to hug Tammy. "It'll be all right, baby girl," she whispered in her ear. "I promise."

"He only did that to—"

"You don't have to explain. I can see through Garrett." She collected the plates. "Come on. Help with the washing up, and then go sit with your Mom."

And tonight, she thought, I'll drug that poisonous father of yours and find out his secrets.

She'd make sure he had more to worry about than his daughter getting Cs in English and History.

$$\overline{}$$

20

In the Still of the Night

$$\overline{}$$

NAT HAD no idea whether Danny Dyson was taking any other medication. She hadn't even thought to check whether he might already be taking sleeping pills. If he was, how much would be too much?

She didn't think he was, though. Danny's one redeeming quality was his devotion to Susannah, and he wouldn't risk not hearing her if she needed him during the night. He had told Nat that the coffee she brought him every night helped him stay alert.

But what if he was taking something else that reacted with the pills?

Too bad, she told herself. There was too much at stake to wonder about things like that.

At nine-thirty, she took in his coffee, laced with four pills. She had even thought about crushing a fifth and mixing it with the icing that topped his slice of carrot cake, but remembering the effect just two pills had had on her, decided against it.

Four would have to be enough.

Her heart beating erratically, she paused at the half-open door to take a deep breath, then tapped lightly and went in.

Danny, half-dozing, jerked upright, and some papers in his hand slid onto the floor.

"Sorry," Nat said. "You were resting."

He waved her comment aside. "Just thought I'd close my eyes for a moment. I was reviewing some household expenses. Things are a little tight right now." He accepted the coffee and pushed some more papers on the table beside him to one side so she could put down the plate with the cake. "This will refuel me."

Nat bent down to pick up the papers from the floor and put them on top of the others. The electric bill, she noted.

Then she saw the keys. Or rather, the end of just one key, visible under the half-dozen accounts that Danny was reviewing.

What she sought was right there, on the table.

The sense of relief almost made her weak at the knees. *Thank you, God,* she said silently. Now she wouldn't have to face searching Danny's pockets.

"I'll see you in the morning," she said and went over to her sister, lying white and frail in the bed, her eyes closed.

"Goodnight, Susannah," she whispered, smoothing a finger over her sister's cheek. "Sleep well."

With a nod to Danny, who was watching her impassively, she turned to go.

"Goodnight, Natalie." Danny raised the cup to his lips and drank, reaching for the slice of cake at the same time.

Tension almost made it impossible to breathe as she walked slowly to the door.

Would he notice anything?

His eyes going to his wife, Danny took a bite of the cake and chewed.

His eyes came back to her, and he watched her leave.

Nothing. Not a frown, no comments about odd tastes.

Nat went to the room she shared with Tammy to wait, talking softly with her niece until the girl's eyes fluttered closed at last.

She gave Danny an hour and then went to the bathroom and flushed the toilet, so she'd have a reason for being up if he was still awake. Then she went to Susannah's room and peeked around the door, ready with a story about thinking she'd heard Susannah call out if her plan had failed.

Danny was lying back in the chair, which was reclined as far back as it would go. He was out like a light. Next to him, the coffee cup and plate were both empty.

Her eyes moved to her sister. Susannah was still deeply asleep.

"Danny?" Nat whispered, moving closer.

He didn't move.

"Danny…? Are you awake?" She edged around his feet to the table beside him, where the papers were once more in disarray.

His eyes remained firmly closed.

At last, things were going her way. It took her only a moment to slide the keys out from under the household accounts, closing her fingers around them tightly so they wouldn't jangle.

With no idea of how much time she had before he surfaced again, she moved quickly to grab the new toner and ream of paper from her room before entering the study. Once inside, she shut the door and locked it. She didn't want Kyle or Garrett to see or hear anything if they got up to use the bathroom.

Her heart still thumping, she switched on the printer and replaced the toner before stacking it with paper.

Now, finally…the filing cabinet. Her fingers sweating, she found the key and slid it into the lock.

Click.

She was in.

She closed her eyes for a beat and waited for calm to descend. This was no different from competition at a high level, she reminded herself; no different to having to control the adrenaline rush before squeezing the trigger to find the target. She had succeeded in elite sport *because* she could create a zone of detached calm and focus.

She would either be caught, or she wouldn't. That was now out of her hands, so she just needed to get on with the job. She'd already planned it: first, a quick scan of the contents of all drawers to identify the most likely-looking files, and second, copy what she needed as fast as she could.

Two hours, max, she had allocated. Surely Danny would be out that long.

Nat pulled open the first drawer and set to work.

Just before three in the morning, Nat, hunched in the chair at Tammy's desk with the desk lamp pulled down low to cast just a small pool of light on the papers in front of her, finally put aside the last of the files she'd copied and stretched tiredly, thinking about what she'd found.

Loretta Paxton, in her anger and misery, had given her a clue about what to look for. Some of what she'd found made sense. Some of it led to more questions, such as how was Danny Dyson making so much money? She intended to find out answers to those questions, and that meant a visit to some of the parishioners, and maybe a trip out to the Retreat built on Rocky Dyson's farm.

Rocky, she had worked out, was kind of like a grown-up Kyle. Mean and sly and not well-regarded by the townsfolk. They saw him as another cross that the wonderful Danny Dyson had to bear.

She now knew better. The relationship between the two brothers, Danny and Rocky, was very similar to that between Garrett and Kyle. One brother charming, bright and talented; the other a follower, not intelligent enough to stay out of trouble.

But the not-so-bright brothers had their uses, as father and son had both discovered.

What she had found was more than enough to tarnish Danny's image in the church community. That, plus the photos she had captured of Garrett and Kyle bullying Tammy, might be enough for Danny to allow her to take Tammy rather than risk exposure.

But it might not. She couldn't take the risk.

If only she had more time. Susannah was getting

weaker, and Nat didn't like to spend too much time away from her…but she *had* to.

She stood up, moving quietly so she wouldn't wake Tammy, and wrapped the photocopied files in a plastic bag before folding them inside a spare lightweight comforter that Tammy kept on the top shelf of her closet. She had already tucked what was left of the paper she'd purchased into the partially-used ream in Danny's office and replaced the original toner cartridge. The new one was in the bottom of her gun bag, wrapped in an old t-shirt. She'd dispose of it in the morning. There should be no visible signs of anyone accessing files in Danny's file cabinet.

The notes she'd made as she read through the files, with a few important names and addresses, she tucked inside a vase on Tammy's dresser. It held vibrant tangerine silk flowers, hand-made by Susannah.

Now she would wait, alert for Susannah's voice, in case she called out before Danny woke. She'd already been in once to replace the keys and had found Danny still out to it, snoring softly in the recliner.

Susannah had been stirring, her eyes barely open, her face creased with pain.

Gently, Nat had given her a drink and more meds and waited until she'd drifted off again. She didn't care if Danny woke now; she would simply tell him that she'd heard Susannah call out.

The hours until morning passed slowly. Nat was glad when the sun rose, and she could get up to start the morning routine.

Now to see if Danny suspected anything.

21

Morning

TAMMY DELAYED AS LONG as possible before going to the kitchen for breakfast. She knew that her aunt wouldn't leave her at her brothers' mercy again, but the memory of the day before was still too raw. Having become used to his sister-in-law's efficiency in the morning, her father had not been impressed to find a dark, empty kitchen.

"Let her sleep," he had ordered, his voice tight. "Tammy, get moving. You know what to do. Garrett, take out the trash. You, Kyle, set the table."

He had fetched the morning newspaper from the porch and sat there like a black cloud while Tammy cooked bacon and cracked eggs into a pan. Garrett, with a guarded glance back to ensure that his father wasn't watching, elbowed Tammy when he opened the cupboard for a new plastic liner, so she stumbled and burned her knuckles on the hot pan. He swiftly stepped away while he tucked the liner into the bin, so when his father looked up at Tammy's yelp of pain, he wasn't even close.

"What *now?*" her father barked at her.

Conscious of Garrett's feral gaze on her, Tammy turned on the faucet and held her hand under the stream of cold water. "Nothing," she said, not looking at either of them. "I burnt my hand."

Her father muttered something that sounded like *useless girl* and went back to his paper.

Garrett smiled at her and said in a patient voice, "Tams, watch that bacon. I think it's burning."

"No, it isn't," she said quickly.

"It had better not be," her father said. "Not at the price we're paying for it."

"It's *not*."

But it *was* burned, just a little on the edges. Although she gave the burned bits to herself, Garrett pretended to have difficulty cutting the meat. He also sighed and reminded her that they all preferred their eggs runny in the middle.

Garrett was masterly at building on little things, Tammy knew. He'd point out one mistake, and then another, and always as though he was genuinely trying to help.

That wasn't, of course, the end of it. She had to wash the dishes, and Garrett nobly offered to help while her father went to tend to her mother. "You can help too," he'd said to his brother with a sly wink.

That had led to her being jostled between the two of them as they cleared the table. When he pretended to steady her, Garrett's iron fingers found a pressure point on her wrist that made her white and breathless with pain. That was followed by a series of low-voiced threats from the two of them while she kept glancing at the door, desperate for her aunt to show up.

She didn't. Tammy finished her chores as quickly as

her brothers would permit, desperate to get out of the house and lose herself at school.

School, where her marks were plummeting, and teachers were looking at her with a mix of pity and disappointment.

Finally, dressed in clothes that hid bruises from her brothers' hands and sporting an undressed burn on her knuckles, she had shaken her aunt awake and raced out the door.

This morning, her aunt was back in the kitchen, and breakfast was on the table when her brothers wandered in. Garrett winked at Tammy, and she looked away, feeling sick.

"Garrett, would you let your father know that breakfast is ready?" her aunt said, putting a plate in front of Tammy. Her hand rested briefly on Tammy's shoulder, giving her a reassuring squeeze.

Garrett didn't miss it, but Tammy knew that he found it amusing. One of his warnings the previous day had been: *"Your new Momma Bear might be showing her claws now, Tammy, but she won't be here much longer. And then we'll have some fun, won't we?"* This had been accompanied by a sharp poke in the ribs.

When he returned from his parents' bedroom, preceding his bleary-eyed, irritable father into the kitchen, he wasn't looking so smug. Tammy stared. Danny Dyson wasn't his usual freshly-showered and dapper self. Still in the previous day's clothes, he looked hungover. He glared around at them all as he thumped down into his seat.

"Sorry," he snapped. "Overslept."

Tammy's aunt put a plate of fragrant, steaming pancakes, drizzled with maple syrup, in front of him.

"It's probably well overdue, Danny," she said quietly. "Weeks without proper sleep has to take its toll, as I found out yesterday—and I'm not up half the night seeing to Susannah as you are."

He grunted, his brows meeting in a scowl.

Nobody said a word for the next fifteen minutes, eating quietly. It was like having a time bomb at the table. Tammy felt the usual weight in her chest magnified. It was always there because of her mother, but when her brothers were toying with her or her father was in a mood, things were ten times worse.

Her aunt stood up to clear the table.

"Tammy," her father snapped. "Help your aunt."

Putting her knife and fork together on her plate with its unfinished pancake, she jumped up to do his bidding.

His eyes went to her plate. "How many times have I told you to finish what's on your plate?"

Stung by the unfairness of his words, Tammy choked back a protest. What was the point? Instead, she mumbled, "Sorry," and picked up the empty plate in front of Kyle to tuck under her own.

Her aunt spoke up. Her voice was quiet but firm. "Danny, Tammy was still eating when you asked her to help. She *was* actually trying to finish it."

Danny's eyes, still glazed, whipped up to her face. "And you know this *how?* You can see into the future?"

Tammy's aunt said nothing for a long moment while she stared at him, and when she did speak, her words were measured. "We're all tired. We're all sad. Let's just try to do our best."

"Well, you know what?" His usual mask of forbearance and friendliness absent, her father glared at his sister-in-law. "I *am* tired. Tired of your unspoken criticism of the way we live and the way I choose to raise my children. If it were not for Susannah's request that you stay, you'd have been out of here weeks ago. I've tried to be charitable, but it's obvious that you don't fit in. I might remind you that *I* am the head of this household." He slammed down his knife and fork and glared at Tammy. "You, clear the table. Put your own plate aside, and then finish your breakfast before you leave. And remember that *I* am the one who makes the rules around here."

His eyes shot to his sons. "As for you two…Garrett, you'll mow the lawn this afternoon. Kyle, you'll stay home instead of going to your uncle's. Weed the garden; it's a jungle."

He ended by stabbing a finger at Tammy's aunt. "And *you'd* better make the most of sitting with your sister instead of shooting at targets like you're some celebrity. Because you're on borrowed time."

Without another word, he stomped out.

For a moment, they were all like statues, and for once, Garrett had nothing to say. His eyes, however, were venomous as he stared after his father.

The whole scene made Tammy faint with dread.

If her aunt left without her, she was going to leave too. She didn't care where she went. Anything would be better than staying here.

"Tammy?"

Her aunt's voice made her look away from Garrett, her fingers still gripping the edge of her plate.

"Sit down and finish your breakfast. And *you,*" she pointed at Garrett, "can take that look off your face when you're around me. Get out of here and get ready for school."

Garrett sneered. "You heard my father. You're on borrowed time."

"That may be so," she said, "but I'm still here, and it would be a pleasure to expose you for who you are. I warned you. Leave Tammy alone."

He just laughed and walked out, followed by Kyle.

Tammy's aunt waited for a beat, and then she moved closer.

"Tammy," she said softly, "I found something."

Tammy stared at her.

Her aunt cast another glance at the door but dropped her voice to a whisper. "I think I've got something on him," she said. Her hand massaged Tammy's back. "I'm sure I'll find more. Just be patient a little longer, sweetie. It will all work out."

22

Following the Trail

AFTER HER BROTHER-IN-LAW finally left for the day, Nat sat with Susannah until she dozed off and then fetched her notes from the night before. She studied them carefully, thinking about the best way to approach the people on her list. She couldn't risk word getting back to Danny that she was asking questions. She still felt cold all over when she thought of how he'd let his true personality emerge at breakfast.

It was the folder labeled *Deceased Estates* that grabbed her attention—naturally enough, after Loretta Paxton's harsh words a few days before. The files all had small adhesive dots stuck in the top right-hand corner. Some were green, some red, and two were orange. At first, she couldn't figure out what they meant, but when she checked the dates, it occurred to her that the two with orange dots were probably still in probate.

The files were organized according to the date parishioners had died and left money or assets to the church. The earliest was dated nine years before.

Nine years, Nat thought. That would figure. She knew that Danny had gradually risen in prominence in the church. When he married 20-year-old Susannah, after a year-long courtship, he had been 29. Well-liked, and already influential, but still youngish.

Nine years ago, on the date of the first bequest, he would have been in his late thirties. Handsome, charming, and calculating. A responsible family man of high standing, with enough energy to have a finger in every pie in the church community.

He'd know which elderly parishioners were vulnerable, which ones to cultivate, so they left him or the church a goodly sum.

But how could she prove anything? People were entitled to leave money to whomever they wished. Family members might challenge the will, maybe get a larger slice of the pie, but they couldn't overturn it.

Not unless there was proof of wrongdoing, and there wasn't anything like that in the files. But when she saw the name *Celia Paxton* on one of the folders, she had sucked in a deep breath.

This was the one she wanted to see: the file for the mother of Loretta Paxton, who had come up to Nat outside the drugstore, saying unforgivable things about Susannah.

The Paxton file had a red dot.

Red, she thought.

Red to signify danger? Red as some kind of alert?

That could be it. And maybe a green dot indicated that everything was fine; all systems go.

And orange for 'pending', if the wills were still in probate.

She could be totally off base, but her gut told her she wasn't. Not when you inserted Loretta Paxton into the equation.

There were only two other files with red dots. Nat made a note of the names: Tina May and David Caraway. Red had to mean something.

Start by pulling a thread, Nat, she told herself. The obvious starting point was the woman from the drugstore, Loretta Paxton.

Nat obeyed Danny's order to stay away from her temporary target range, and although she hated leaving her, she didn't spend the time sitting with her sister either. When Grace Tennant tiptoed into Susannah's bedroom, raising her eyebrows in a silent query, Nat put her finger to her lips and motioned her outside.

"She seems very tired today," she told her quietly. "I don't think she's up to conversation. Would you mind sitting with her while I take care of some errands?"

"Of course, I will." Grace looked at her keenly. "You're not looking so good yourself. Why don't you take a few hours out? Go and have a cup of coffee overlooking the park, maybe do some mindless shopping?" Then she pulled a wry face and laughed. "No, you're not the mindless shopping type."

Nat had to smile. "You've got me there. No, I just have a few things to pick up." Struck by inspiration, she added a rueful laugh. "Although if I go to the drugstore, I might check to make sure that Loretta Paxton isn't lying in wait. She, uh, doesn't seem to like our family."

Grace narrowed her eyes. "Loretta? Why? What did she say?"

"Oh, pretty much that Susannah was no better than she ought to be and that the Dyson family has ruined her life." The memory of it still stung, although Nat knew that Susannah was being judged because of her husband's actions. "It was unfair. Susannah's not like that."

"She certainly isn't." Grace patted her on the arm. "Don't let it get to you. Loretta is just sore because her mother didn't leave it all to her."

"She accused Danny of manipulating her mother into changing her will, with Susannah's knowledge."

"Yes, she's said the same thing to many people." Grace sighed. "She has five children, and she has exhausted her savings to help them. They always want more, and my personal opinion is that Celia Paxton left most of her money to the church to force her grandchildren to stand on their own two feet. "

Nat hesitated and then ventured, "Do *you* believe it was Danny's influence?"

"Absolutely not," Grace said firmly. "Danny is a charmer; there's no doubt about that. Some people might see that as being manipulative, granted, but everything's above board. Any time a parishioner leaves something to the church—or to him, for looking after their welfare—he's stringent about running it by the church legal team. Terrence Busby puts everything through a magnifying glass, and he's bent over backward to be fair to any other heirs. I know, I'm on the church council."

"Terrence Busby?" Nat raised her eyebrows.

"Solicitor. Third generation in this town." Grace

smiled at her. "Don't you worry about it anymore, Nat. I'd have a word to Loretta myself, but I'd be wasting my breath. She ended up with enough for her needs, don't you worry."

"It wasn't her needs that she seemed concerned about."

"Well, it's her choice what she does with her money. I have to say that I'm of the same mind as Celia. Children need to make their own way in life."

Not always, Nat thought, picturing Tammy's haunted eyes. Sometimes they needed help.

"Anyway," she said, "I'd better run. I want to be back before the kids get home."

As if she had read her mind, Grace asked, "How's Tammy coping?" Her face was so sympathetic that Nat fought down an urge to tell her that Tammy was *not* coping, and there was no way she could make her own way in life with a father like Danny Dyson and a brother like Garrett.

But now was not the time.

"Not so good," she said. "You can imagine what it's like for a girl her age to know she's going to lose her mother. But she'll come through."

"With your help, she will," Grace said. "The parishioners will all keep an eye on her, on the whole family, but it's not the same as having a mother around. It's a pity you can't stay." Immediately, she waved her words away. "Sorry. Not my place to say."

"I'll do my best for her," Nat promised grimly. "Anyway, I'd better be going."

It was in the car, on the way to town, that it clicked.

Terrence Busby. The older man she had seen with Danny; the one he hadn't introduced. She'd thought he'd called him Lawrence, but it must have been Terrence.

A solicitor who came to meet him at his house, rather than at a legal office…

She had to talk to Loretta Paxton.

23

Red for Alert

THERE WERE QUITE a few Paxtons listed in the phone book, but Nat couldn't find any Lorettas. She started working her way through the ones that were there and finally hit pay dirt.

"Loretta? That's my mom," said a woman listed under *Paxton, FE & JJ.* "You'll find her listed under Pamela. She calls herself by her middle name." She broke off to yell at a child whining in the background, then came back to say, "Sorry, I have to go." Abruptly, the call was terminated.

Good, thought Nat. She much preferred the idea of showing up at her door without giving Loretta a chance to 'don't come'.

It was a good plan in theory, but nobody was home. After pressing an ancient door chime and hearing nothing, and then getting no response to her repeated knocks, Nat let herself in through the lopsided gate and walked around to the back of the house in case Loretta was in the yard.

The place was long past due for a new coat of paint,

and the lawn was long and unkempt. Nat did some calculations. Celia had been 91 when she died, so she guessed that Loretta would be in her sixties. Her five children were probably in their thirties and forties. It didn't appear that any of them did much to help their mother around the house.

Nat looked at her watch. She had almost an hour and a half before Grace was due to leave; she could afford to wait a while.

She sat in her car, thinking about Danny and Garrett and Kyle and how different they were to Tammy and Susannah.

Tammy was like her mother, sweet and kind and talented, but with the ability to see people far more clearly than Susannah. Not that she'd had much choice. She'd had to understand at a very young age that good looks and charm could mask corruption and hatred.

She deserved better.

Nat turned her mind to some of the other things she'd found in Danny's filing cabinet. Bank statements, for a start, from a bank in another town. She didn't know whether he was clever enough to hide more accounts offshore, and she didn't really care. She wanted nothing from Danny Dyson but his daughter.

The bank balance was sizable, making nonsense of his claims that his family had to live modestly. A lot of his income seemed to come from the Dyson Retreat that he'd established on his brother's farm. Rocky, it seemed, was paid a generous monthly rent for the land on which the Retreat had been built; enough, so he didn't have to do any farming.

So what was it that Kyle did out there when 'helping out' his uncle?

He had no skills, no training that would be of use to the Retreat, which seemed to take in troubled people of all descriptions, judging by the brochures Danny kept in his office. He charged what seemed to Nat to be exorbitant sums for his 'guests' (as the brochure described them: not 'clients' or 'patients'), and the staff included a doctor, nurse, spiritual advisor, and various therapists.

Call her cynical, but by dubbing the place a 'retreat', Danny Dyson could do what he liked there. It appeared to have links to the church but was privately run.

There was so much to find out, and she was running out of time.

Nat was brought out of her reverie by a car turning into the driveway. Loretta Paxton got out and shaded her eyes with one hand against the bright late-morning sun, trying to make out who was behind the wheel of the car waiting outside her house. Nat knew she wouldn't be able to see through the darkened glass.

Here goes, she thought, opening the door. She wasn't expecting a warm welcome.

Loretta's face changed as soon as she realized who her visitor was. She took a step back, looking wary.

"Hi, Loretta." Nat slowed her footsteps and stopped a body length away from the other woman, smiling to show that she wasn't there to make trouble.

"What do you want?"

Nat took heart from the fact that the words sounded more curious than challenging, although there was a hint of defiance there.

"I know you have issues with my family," she said, deciding quickly that there was no room here for niceties. "But if you could spare a few minutes to talk,

I'd really appreciate it. I'd like to hear your point of view."

Loretta didn't smile back. Suspicion lurked at the back of her eyes. "It's all a bit late now, isn't it? A condition of the settlement was that I didn't take further action and that I didn't talk about it. I shouldn't even have said anything to you the other day."

"But you did," Nat said. "And I'm glad you did." She stopped, wondering how to reach Loretta. "You probably know I'm here to look after my sister until she passes. But the Susannah I grew up with would not ruin someone else's life for financial gain."

Loretta's lips twisted. "The Susannah you grew up with must have changed."

"I don't think so. I really don't. But…." Nat sighed. "Please? I'm just trying to make sense of what's going on. If you could tell me about your mother, about Danny and the church, it would help. And I promise I won't mention to anyone that you talked to me."

For a moment Loretta stood, irresolute, but then she seemed to slump. She sighed. "All right. Why not? Nobody *else* listens." She turned and pulled a few shopping bags out of the back seat of her car, slammed the door, and motioned towards the front door with her head. "Come in, then."

Loretta leaned back on a worn sofa and folded her arms, waiting while Nat settled herself in a facing armchair. Clearly, whatever she had done with the settlement money, none of it had been used for her own comfort. The furniture was all old, and from where she sat, Nat could see a kitchen cupboard door that hung slightly askew.

"Are you going to start, or am I?" Loretta asked. Now that she had invited Nat into her home, she seemed less adversarial.

"All I know," Nat said, "is what you told me in the drugstore. Since I got here, I've just been taking care of Susannah and the boys. I don't really know much about the church, apart from talking to the ladies on the care roster. I know nothing about your Mom. So how about you tell me what you think I should know?"

Loretta took a while to answer. She took a breath as though to start, and then stopped and looked to one side while she gathered her thoughts. Finally, she said, "If I'm going to talk to you, I can't mince words."

"I don't want you to."

"Right." Another breath. "In that case, I think Danny Dyson is a crook who uses his position in the church to worm his way into people's lives and then takes what he wants. I know I've got a personal stake in it, but it's not just me. You should take a look at the others who have left everything to the church or to *him*." She stole a quick glance at Nat before looking away. "The Caraways and the Mays challenged bequests made to him but got nowhere, same as me. Thanks to Terrence Busby." Her final words came out in a rush. "And I still have a hard time believing that Susannah was oblivious to it all."

Nat nodded, her mind working furiously. Would she get more out of Loretta if she shared her own feelings about Danny?

No, she couldn't take the risk. If Loretta was hurting enough to confront someone in public, then she'd be all too likely to repeat anything Nat said about her brother-in-law.

"Can you tell me what happened?" she said. "What your mother said about Danny and the church, perhaps? Or did the will come as a total shock to you?"

Loretta gave a derisive laugh. "A shock? No. We could see it coming. My mother talked non-stop about Danny Dyson towards the end. How much he cared about people, how he put almost everything he earns back into the church, what good work they do." She looked at Nat challengingly. "Mom went on and on about how rare it was to see someone actually practice what they preached, about how Danny and his family wore recycled clothes—that's how *he* refers to it, not second-hand, but "recycled". She'd tell us how he'd never bought a new car and how that Retreat of his changes lives and brings people back to an under-standing of what's important in life. Well, I've heard what he charges people to go there, and in my opinion, what's important in life to Danny Dyson is lining his hip pocket."

Nat thought about the size of the bank balance in an out-of-town bank and found herself nodding in agreement.

"What do you know about the Retreat?" she asked quickly before Loretta moved away from the subject.

"Not much. Most of my time has been taken up fighting for my inheritance." Resentment sparked in her eyes again. "The Retreat…I know a few people who have paid for family members to go there. It's all touchy-feely stuff as far as I can make out, but there's a doctor there to prescribe anti-depressants and the like. I have a friend…" she hesitated and said, "No names."

"Of course."

"I have a friend who re-mortgaged her home to send her son there. He was unemployed, running with the wrong crowd, and after she went to Danny Dyson for advice, she gave her boy an ultimatum. Either he checked into the Retreat and went through the program, or she'd ask him to move out and withdraw all financial support. He was supposed to stay for eight weeks, but it ended up being closer to four months. When he came out, she could see no change, and then he left town— after cleaning her out." Loretta smiled grimly. "When she finally started asking more questions about the kind of program being offered, it was all too late. Danny suddenly became too busy to talk to her."

"I've seen the brochures that Danny has in the office," Nat said slowly, "but there's not much real information on them. Plenty of glowing testimonials from guests, I saw."

"Precisely," Loretta said. "The Retreat recommends that people come in for a consultation to have a program tailored for their needs. Which, of course, gives Danny a chance to talk them into it. He's very good at making people feel they need to do more to support what the church is doing, whether it's about leaving a bequest or using the Retreat."

Finally, Nat was beginning to get a clearer picture of her brother-in-law's influence and activities. The question was, how could she use this against him? It didn't appear that he'd broken the law. No doubt he took care that he didn't.

Snatching at straws, she asked, "What's this Retreat like?"

"I can only tell you what I've heard from Therese."

Loretta didn't appear to notice that she'd used her friend's name. "I think there's a separate building, fenced off, for people withdrawing from drugs or alcohol. She said she grilled Danny about that because she didn't want her son coming into contact with people who might encourage him to use drugs. She realizes now that she was blind, of course; he was already using." Loretta closed her eyes, evidently trying to picture the place. "Danny gave her a tour when he was trying to talk her into sending her son there. From memory, there's the main building, and a pool, massage therapy rooms, meeting rooms, recreation facilities, and so on. From what my friend says about her conversations with Danny, he welcomes anyone trying to find meaning in life or get back on track. Pregnant teenagers, anger management… one size fits all." She rolled her eyes. "It's just a money machine."

Nat thought of the mother and teenager Danny had been counseling and wondered if the girl was the latest target. She'd try to find out.

"Anyway, back to Mom," Loretta said. "We tried to talk to her when we could see where it was leading. I'd heard about others who'd left their money to the church, so I was concerned. I tried to explain that the inheritance could make the difference between some of her grandchildren keeping their heads above water and going under, but she didn't want to know. Said she'd leave me enough for my own needs, but my kids were adults, and they could earn their way like everyone else. Bone lazy, she said." Her lip trembled. "They're not. They've just had a hard time. I've helped as much as I can, but now I can't do any more unless I sell this place and move in with one of them."

"I think you need to consider your own security," Nat said before she could stop herself. "It's a big step, giving up your home."

"And I wouldn't even have to think about doing it if I'd got my inheritance," Loretta said acidly.

Nat felt helpless. "I'm really sorry. I know it's no help, but for what it's worth…."

Loretta's eyes narrowed, and she cocked her head to one side. "No, it's no help, but I can't help wondering why you came, after what I said the other day. Could it be you don't like your sister's husband any more than I do?"

Nat sidestepped that one, hoping her face didn't give her away. "It's probably more a case of sticking up for my sister. Susannah hasn't got a devious bone in her body."

A tiny smile crept onto Loretta's face. "You *don't* like him."

"I don't like any form of manipulation," Nat said, "if that's what happened."

"Oh, that's what happened all right." Loretta tapped her fingers on the arm of the sofa, still staring at Nat, before seeming to come to some sort of decision. "Excuse me for a moment."

She left the room, and a few moments later, Nat heard the sound of her voice. The words were indistinguishable, but from the stop-start conversation, it was clear she was talking on the phone.

When she came back, she had a folded piece of paper in her hand. "Here." She offered it to Nat. "I just spoke to my friend. If you want to, you can hear the full story from Therese." She shrugged. "I don't know whether anything will come of it, but we'd both be happy to see Danny Dyson get his comeuppance."

Nat took it and then offered her hand. "I can't promise anything."

"I know that."

"Please don't tell anyone I came to see you."

"Fine, as long as *you* don't tell anyone I talked to you."

24

Chase

FOUR NIGHTS LATER, sitting in a dimly-lit bar, Nat was so wired she felt like she might explode. She shouldn't be here; she should be at home, on call for her sister.

Susannah was clearly getting weaker by the day. Almost by the *hour*. Nat could tell from the hopelessness in Danny's eyes that he'd seen it too, but a heartbreaking conversation with Dr. Morris had clinched it.

A couple of weeks at the most, the doctor had said gently. But more likely less. In her face, in her eyes, Nat saw the truth.

They were down to days.

Susannah didn't have the energy to talk much anymore, and Tammy barely managed to choke down a few mouthfuls of food at mealtimes. When her father snapped at her, she simply looked at him and said nothing. She no longer seemed to care what he said or did.

When Nat scanned through the photocopied information she had about Danny, and a few scribbled notes after talking to people, she felt despair. What did she have, really? Bank statements that showed a healthy income that he was clearly hiding from his family and the church, and a few accusations that he had exerted undue influence on vulnerable older parishioners. She had talked to Loretta, and her friend Therese Gilmore, and a few other people with whom they'd quietly arranged meetings. It was clear that not everyone connected with the church was a Danny Dyson fan, but they were a tiny minority. Danny had a great deal of power and influence and hundreds of loyal followers.

One throwaway comment by Therese had kept worrying at her mind. *I gave Chase every chance, but when I found out he'd been going back out to the Retreat to work for that no-good Rocky Dyson, that was it. That place isn't even a working farm anymore. Whatever he was doing for Rocky, it was probably on the shady side of the law.*

A month later, Chase was gone, along with his mother's car and a good chunk of her savings. Therese, furious, had confronted Danny Dyson rather than going to the police, but Danny was adamant that Chase was lying about working on the farm. The best thing that Therese could do, he said sadly, was to let him go and learn his own life lessons the hard way. They had all tried, but….

Tuning him out, Therese had risen to her feet and walked out without another word. She decided to move on from both her son Chase *and* Danny Dyson. She'd heard that Chase was back in town but hadn't attempted to contact him.

For a couple of days, Nat mulled over what Therese had said. She toyed with the idea of going out to the farm to see what she could find but quickly dismissed that idea. Rocky wouldn't tell her anything useful, if he agreed to see her at all, and she didn't know what she was looking for anyway.

She had to talk to Chase Gilmore.

Finally, desperation saw her calling her solicitor back in Chesterfield to ask if he could put her in contact with a private detective close to Baton Rouge. After a couple of questions, he made some calls and finally gave her three names. Two were willing to give her missing-person case priority for a premium fee. She hired the one who said he'd start right away.

Since Therese's son, Chase, hadn't bothered covering his tracks, the task was ridiculously easy. Nat was in possession of Chase's contact details and some background information within twelve hours. Nat called him, gave him a fake name, and offered him five hundred bucks for fifteen minutes of his time. When he started asking questions, she promised him another five hundred at the end of the conversation if she got what she wanted.

Luckily, Chase seemed to be the type who didn't perceive any kind of threat from a female. The prospect of a thousand bucks for a quick meeting finally persuaded him.

Now she was sitting by herself in a quiet corner, watching a kid with a bodybuilder's physique and plenty of attitude sauntering towards her.

When he stopped in front of her, she took the initiative before he could open his mouth.

"You're Chase," she said, keeping her voice level and authoritative. "I've seen photos. Sit down."

He shoved his hands in his pockets and stood there for a good ten seconds before taking a seat, just to show her that he was only doing it because *he* wanted to do it. "And who are *you*, exactly? Tina Carter, you said? Is that your real name?"

Nat smiled, almost feeling sorry for him. She'd faced down tougher opponents than him a million times. "I'm someone who's willing to pay well for information. That's all you need to know," she said pleasantly. Her thoughts turned briefly to the background information on Chase Gilmore provided by the investigator. *He just got hired as a runner/enforcer for Ray "Fats" Bishop. Small stuff so far, but the cops are keeping an eye on him.* She leaned back in her chair, folding her hands together on the table, looking relaxed. "I'm sure Fats doesn't tell everyone who *you* are."

He went still. She could see the wheels turning in his mind: did his new boss know about this meeting? Had Fats told her where to find him? He hadn't been in the organization long enough to work it out, and he certainly wasn't high enough in the pecking order to ask anyone else.

"Don't worry," she said, keeping her eyes steadily on his. "I know how to keep my mouth shut. Nobody will hear from me about what you do for Fats. As long as I find out what I want to know." She lifted her hands so he could see the envelope underneath them. "There's five hundred in this envelope. You talk for fifteen minutes, answer my questions, and it's yours."

"You said there'd be more at the end."

"That depends on the quality of the information."

"How do I know you're not with the cops?"

"I don't care what you do, Chase. I have my own agenda, and it means operating outside the law. I don't want the cops in on this any more than you do. You want the money or not?"

"Maybe," he said cautiously. "What do you want to know?"

"Danny Dyson," she said, her voice mild. "Rocky Dyson. Anything you can tell me."

His lips curled in a sneer at Danny's name, but he looked wary when she mentioned Rocky. He shifted uncomfortably in his seat. "They going to find out about this?"

"Not from me," she said. "I told you, I'm outside the law. First, Danny Dyson. Tell me about this program of his."

He laughed and swore. "Effing load of crap. He—"

"You can leave the swearing out of it. What was the daily program?"

He rolled his eyes. "A meeting with a therapist. Fifteen minutes of being preached at. Then relaxation and meditation, which meant I could swim or work out or make cane baskets, if that's what I felt like. I was supposed to examine my own conscience, work out what I really wanted out of life, empower myself and a load of other crap. Do you really want to know?"

"What did you *actually* do there?"

"Swam worked on my tan, worked out, watched TV." He smirked. "And figured out how to make contact with," he made wiggling quotation marks with his fingers, "those recovering from *substance abuse*."

"Did you have access to drugs?"

"Yeah. Not *officially*, of course. Saint Danny wouldn't have allowed that."

"So he didn't sanction drugs coming onto the premises?"

"You kidding? What part of "Saint Danny" don't you understand?"

Pity, she thought. That would have given her something to work on. "Were you permitted to leave the Retreat?"

"Not officially." He grinned at her again.

"So you did. How?"

"Danny's son Kyle. And his brother Rocky."

"How did you meet them?"

"We were free to move around the grounds." He nodded at the envelope, partly visible under her fingertips. "That must be five hundred bucks worth."

She looked at her watch. "In six minutes? I don't think so." Her eyes met his again. "I need something on Danny Dyson. Or his brother, or his son. But it's got to be good."

He opened his mouth and then closed it again. She could see the indecision in his eyes, and she could see the moment he decided to test her.

Finally, he leaned forward, leering at her. "Make it five grand, and I'll give you something."

Her heart jumped, but she shook her head. "Five grand? For that, you'd have to have seen them commit murder and hide the body."

"Murder, no," he said. "Hidden bodies, yes."

That made her mouth drop open.

Chase laughed at her expression. "Five grand?"

"I'll need proof."

"I've got names."

Nat drummed her fingers on the table. Names were one thing, but the proof was essential. "We don't have a deal if I don't get proof."

"Names are all you need. Give those names to the right people, and the Dysons are toast."

She hesitated. Could she trust him? The very

thought of it made her laugh. The words "trust" and "Chase Gilmore" didn't belong in the same sentence.

But Tammy… Tammy's safety was worth five grand. What else did she have to spend her money on?

She made a decision. "I have one thousand with me. Tell me what happened, give me those names, and if I can do something with it, I'll give you the rest within a week."

He frowned. "How do I know you'll be good for it?"

"What have you got to lose? At worst, you get a grand for fifteen minutes of your time. But you don't have to worry, Chase. I keep *my* word."

He didn't miss the inference, and for a moment, his face darkened. Then he put his hand out. "Five hundred first, and I tell you."

"Trusting soul, aren't you?" She pushed the envelope towards him and watched while he checked the ten fifties inside.

"Show me the other five hundred."

Nat smiled at him unpleasantly. Self-important little toad. "Sure." She unhooked her bag from the back of the chair and, with a quick look around, opened the flap and let him see her move the gun to one side to reveal a second envelope. She drew it out with her fingers and opened it so he could see the money.

He glanced at it; then his eyes returned to the gun. "You licensed to carry that?"

"Yes. And I'm an exceptional shot. Now, stop messing about. What have you got? Spill."

25

Exit Plan

Back at the Dyson home, Tammy's mother hadn't spoken or moved for hours. She breathed so shallowly that Tammy, her heart seizing in panic, had to lean closer several times to check that she was still alive.

She couldn't bear to think that one day soon.... No. She *wouldn't* think of it.

Tammy ran her fingers gently over the back of her mother's hand and forced herself to think about the future. *Trust me,* her aunt had said, but Tammy had seen the increasing strain in her eyes and knew that she was getting worried. The day before, Tammy had not been able to contain herself any longer and had whispered to her when the lights went out in their room. "Aunt Nat, have you found anything more yet?"

Her aunt hadn't ducked the question. After a brief silence, Tammy heard a sigh and her aunt said, "I've found a few things he wouldn't want to be made public. But I'll be honest. Tams: I haven't got enough yet to make him give you up. But I will."

Tammy swallowed hard. "Do you think you'll find it…in time?"

"I'm going to do my darnedest." Her aunt tried to sound confident, but Tammy didn't miss the underlying stress. "If not, I'll ask him if you can come to visit for a short break since I won't be seeing you much anymore. I'll keep you with me as long as I can…until I can have you forever."

Fighting to keep her voice even, Tammy said, "He'll say no."

"Maybe not. I'll use the photos as…a persuader."

As blackmail, Tammy thought. It wouldn't work. Her father was too powerful. If her aunt didn't find anything more, she would have to stay here with her father, with…. *Garrett.* She knew it.

Her eyes went back to her mother. Sitting here tonight, watching her fade away, Tammy had finally come to a decision. She was going to run away. Right after they laid her mother to rest, she would wait for her chance and disappear.

She knew where her father kept the emergency fund; they all did. It was there so he could show generosity when one of his struggling parishioners came to see him. He would occasionally give someone enough money to pay a bill or put food on the table. There were three hundred dollars there, enough to cover several deserving cases in one day if necessary. As soon as possible, after he dipped into it, he replaced it.

Wonderful, generous Danny Dyson, who treated everyone in his church family as though they were *his* family.

She would leave an IOU, tell him she would pay it back one day.

In six months, maybe a year, when they had stopped looking for her, she would finally join her aunt, beg her not to tell her father where she was.

Tammy thought more about her plan, her eyes on her mother's pale face. She'd been to enough funeral services at the church to be able to look ahead. After the graveside service, when everyone went back to the house, she would look for an opportunity to slip away. She could leave a backpack out near where Aunt Nat had set up her targets and make her way to the road from there.

She'd have to hitch-hike, she decided. There was no other way. If she caught a bus, someone at the bus station might remember her.

She instantly thought, *Hitch-hiking. Dad will be furious*, and her pulse raced in fear at the thought. Then she reminded herself that she'd never have to see him again, so it didn't matter.

"Tammy?"

She jumped at the sound of her father's voice, feeling her pulse leap. It was almost as though he could read her mind.

This time, he seemed distracted. With his eyes on Susannah, lying so still in the bed, he simply said, "Time's up," and stood waiting for her to get up and give him her seat.

Marginally heartened by his apathy, she took a deep breath. "Will you come to get me if she gets worse?"

"If that happens, I'll wake *all* of you." His eyes finally went to her. "Where's your aunt?"

She leaned over and kissed her mother on the forehead before she answered, so she wouldn't have to look at him. "I don't know. Isn't she here?"

"Would I have asked you if she was? She didn't say where she was going?"

Tammy shook her head. "No."

He grunted. "All right then. Done your homework?"

Homework, she thought, with a final glance at her mother. How could he even mention it with her mother so sick?

She hated him.

"No," she said, and then it burst out before she could stop it. "Mom's *dying.* What do I care about homework?"

His eyes narrowed. "That sort of insubordination is not appropriate, Tammy. I've told you before; we're all hurting. Grow *up.*"

"Is that what you tell people in your counseling sessions? To *grow up?*" Tammy could see from his face that she was way, way overstepping the boundaries, but she didn't care. "You're nice to everyone but your own family."

"Stop it!" He seized her arm and shook her, his face going red. "You—"

From the bed, they heard a slight noise of distress, and Tammy caught movement from the corner of her eye.

Her mother's eyelids fluttered weakly.

"Are you happy now?" her father ground out in an undertone and pushed her away. "Go to your room. We'll discuss this later." He sat in the armchair next to the bed and took his wife's hand in his, and his voice became soft and soothing. "It's all right, Susannah. It's all right."

Tammy went to her room, letting the tears of frustration and grief spill over.

Two hours later, Nat came home. Tammy heard her talking to her father and his low voice in return. She tiptoed to the door and cracked it, listening. They were in the sitting room, not her mother's bedroom.

"… needed a break, all right?" her aunt said. "I knew that Tammy would be here, and you."

"*Now* you need a break? When Susannah is in her final *hours?* My opinion of you was right all along."

Her aunt's voice sharpened. "I'm not concerned with your opinion of me, Danny."

"Oh, I know *that.* I've known that ever since I married your sister. And now your attitude is influencing Tammy. She was unforgivably rude tonight."

"She's a thirteen-year-old girl who's about to lose her mother! I'm surprised she's held it together as well as she has."

"She's been taught better. Now she's upsetting Susannah."

"Tammy wouldn't do that deliberately. What did you say to her?"

"You're inferring it was *my* fault?"

"You're hard on her, Danny. I don't know why you can't see that."

There was silence for a moment, and when her father spoke again, it was clear that he'd taken a few seconds to pull himself together. Using what she thought of as his 'counseling' voice, he said in measured tones, "We're never going to see eye to eye on that. And really, it has nothing to do with you. When you leave, I'll be raising my daughter the way she should be raised. She'll be strong and resilient, and she'll know the rewards of serving others. And that's all I have to say on the subject."

Tammy heard his footsteps walking back to the bedroom. A few seconds later came the light *snick* of the bathroom door shutting after her aunt.

Her heart felt heavy. If her aunt had needed to go out, to get some space from them all, she must be feeling more stressed than usual.

Which meant that she was getting nowhere.

Tammy went back to bed, slid back under the sheets, and turned her face to the wall. When her aunt came into the darkened room, she feigned sleep. She didn't need to hear any more promises, however well-meant.

26

Dark Days

OVER THE NEXT FEW DAYS, a heavy weight of expectancy and dread hung over the household. Dr. Morris had taken to visiting each evening; Susannah needed large amounts of morphine to dull the pain and was now barely aware of the people around her.

Then, just after midday on a bright spring day, she finally took her last breath. Knowing the end was close, they were all sitting in her room, waiting.

Tammy had been taking every breath with her mother. In, out, in, out…*in*. Sometimes the 'in' was so slight it almost wasn't detectable.

And then it wasn't there at all.

Her father bent over his wife and studied her face, his face rigid. Then his shoulders slumped, and his head fell onto her chest.

"She's gone," he said, his voice muffled.

Tammy felt her aunt's arms come around her from behind, and a light kiss pressed on the top of her head. She closed her eyes, her lips trembling.

Her beautiful mother was gone, really gone.

Now she was truly alone.

The next few days passed in a blur. Tammy, after sobbing for what felt like hours in her aunt's arms, dully set about following whatever instructions her father handed out. She felt like she was inhabiting someone else's body, putting one foot in front of the other, carrying out routine tasks. People brought casseroles and salads and cakes, but she barely touched any of them. Her father ate mechanically, not appearing to notice what she did.

With so many people coming and going from the house, and instructions from their father to have the yard and garden looking pristine, Garrett and Kyle were too busy to torment her. Nobody noticed when she slipped out to hide her backpack up near the makeshift shooting range.

Her aunt kept casting worried looks her way, but she was tied up talking to the women from the church and others who called in to pay their respects, as well as making sure everyone was adequately fed. She didn't badger Tammy about eating, and for a change, her father didn't say anything about finishing the food on her plate.

Why would he? Just a few more days and he could rule the household the way he wanted to.

Well, she wouldn't be part of that household.

The morning before the funeral, her aunt came to find her. Tammy was folding laundry and putting it away.

"Come with me, Tams," she said. "You need new shoes for tomorrow."

Tammy looked at her, surprised. "I have shoes."

"Nothing appropriate for a funeral," said her aunt, pitching her voice loud enough to be overheard. "I know your black shoes are pinching your feet; you'll need new ones anyway, so you might as well get them now and look decent for tomorrow."

Since the black shoes in question fit her perfectly well, Tammy realized that it was an excuse for them both to go into town. For a moment, her heart leaped. Did this mean that her aunt had finally found something?

"Come on." Nat nodded at the laundry basket. "You can finish that later. We need to take the opportunity to go now while it's quiet."

They walked out to the car without speaking, but as soon as they were heading down the driveway, Nat spoke. "You've probably been wondering how my investigation is progressing."

Her voice didn't sound excited, and Tammy's hopes died. "You haven't found anything."

"I have some good leads. *Really* good ones. But it'll take time to follow up. I've hired a private detective."

Astounded, Tammy swung her head to look at her aunt. "A *detective?*"

"There's only so much I can do by myself. He's a retired police officer, so he has some good contacts."

"What's his name?"

"Maybe it's best you don't know that." Nat turned onto the road into town and then reached across to pat

Tammy on the knee. "I can tell you're losing hope, Tams, but you mustn't. It might take time, but this way, we'll be sure that we've got something on him."

Tammy stared straight ahead. "How much time?"

"If I knew, I'd tell you. It could be a few days. It could be a few weeks."

"What if it's longer?"

Her aunt heaved a ragged sigh. "I know every day you have to spend with your father and brothers will be a nightmare, but I need to make sure that whatever we've got on him will stick. And what I've got so far… well, it might tarnish your father by association, Tams, but I wouldn't put it past him to deny it all or twist it and come out of it smelling like roses. You know what he's like."

"So, he's going to get out of it. And I'll have to stay."

"If we do it all legally, he might wriggle out of it, yes. That's why I'm *not* going through the usual channels."

Tammy looked at her aunt, puzzled. "I don't know what you mean."

"Your father has worked hard for his position in the community. He's trusted, and he's powerful. He won't want to give that up, so I'm looking for something to hold over him without going public. Something strong enough to force him to give you up, rather than risk exposure."

Tammy could understand that. "Blackmail."

"Yes, I guess you'd have to call it that."

"But what *is* it?" Tammy asked. "What is this private detective doing?"

"When it's all over, I'll tell you—but for now, I think it's best if you don't know what I'm doing. That way, if anyone puts pressure on you, you don't have to pretend."

Tammy leaned her head against the window. "When are you leaving?"

"Your father wants me out the day after tomorrow."

"Did you ask if I could go with you for a few weeks?"

"I'm waiting for the right moment. I *will* ask him. Right now, we barely tolerate each other." Again, she reached across and squeezed Tammy's knee. "I'll go home, get your room ready for you. And fly down to bring you back when everything's in place." She gave a short laugh. "Even if I have to kidnap you."

27

The Funeral

THE DAY of the funeral dawned bright and clear. Tammy put on the black dress the church ladies had given her and her new black shoes and tied back her hair, and then sat numbly waiting for the black cars to arrive to take them to the service.

The cars took them to a packed church service and then to the cemetery to watch her mother's white casket being lowered into the ground. At the wake, dozens of people hugged her and told her she was a brave girl, and her father was a wonderful man, and she would be all right, but they'd be there for her if she needed anything. Tammy just kept nodding and saying, "Thank you," and tuned everyone out.

She was standing in a corner holding a plate with an uneaten sandwich, half-listening to her aunt conversing with Grace, when her father walked up to them.

Pitching his voice loud enough for people nearby to hear, he said in heartfelt tones, "Thank you, Natalie, for being so good to us in Susannah's last days. My children and I will never forget your kindness. It's a pity you have to leave, but we'll make sure that we keep you updated. Naturally, you'll be welcome in our house at any time."

Natalie looked at him and put down the tray of snacks she had been offering around to the mourners present. "Thank you, Danny. It's been a privilege to tend to my sister in her last days. May I see you privately for a moment?" She smiled at him neutrally, aware of nearby eyes and ears.

"Of course."

Probably nobody but Tammy would pick up on the cynical twist to his mouth as he spoke. She knew instinctively that he was looking forward to the opportunity of telling Natalie exactly what he really thought of her.

Was her aunt going to have one last attempt to talk him into letting Tammy spend a few weeks with her?

Nat put a hand on her shoulder. "You stay here, Tammy. I'll be back in a moment." She handed the tray to Grace. "Would you mind passing these around for me?"

Grace took the tray and looked at the half-dozen mini sausage rolls. "There are more warming in the oven; I'll get those." She headed off.

Watching the retreating backs of her aunt and her father, Tammy had felt her eyes fill. Then an arm slid around her shoulders, and Tammy, feeling her flesh crawl, knew who it was before he said a word. She tensed.

Garrett's smarmy voice whispered in her ear. "So, Tammy, your protector is leaving. No more hiding behind good old aunt Nat. It's going to be so nice, just the four of us together, isn't it?" He squeezed her shoulder while Tammy swallowed, staring at her feet.

"Only an hour or so, and everyone will be gone.

Tomorrow, we wave goodbye to Auntie Nat. *Then* we'll have some things to settle."

"Tammy! Garrett!" Another voice broke in, and Tammy glanced up to see Marie, one of the women from the church who had helped take care of her mother for the past few months. "I just need to say how sorry I am for your loss." She reached over and patted Garrett on the cheek. "Garrett, it's so nice to see you comforting your sister." She took Tammy's hand and covered it warmly with her other one. "You make such a lovely picture, the two of you—like peas in a pod. Susannah would be proud of both of you." Marie's eyes teared up. "Be strong. You'll get through this. And I'm just a phone call away if you need help."

Garrett smiled at her, somehow managing to look sweet and kind, as though he was fighting his sorrow to make his sister feel better. "Thank you."

Marie hugged them both and moved away.

"And that, Tammy," Garrett said in a voice so soft that only she could hear, "is why nobody would ever believe you. I'm your loving big brother." He tipped up her chin and smiled into her eyes, aware of the many eyes watching them. "Catch up with you later, sweetheart."

Shaking, Tammy watched him move away while the eyes of every female in the room gravitated towards him. He might be only seventeen, but already, Garrett looked the perfect man. Fit, muscled, handsome, and utterly charming.

She could never win against Garrett.

She found a chair in a corner and sat there, nodding and smiling at people and murmuring a few words when she had to, but with her mind whirling, planning her options. She *couldn't* stay. She would run, rather than stay here even one day to endure whatever torture her brothers had planned.

And then Aunt Nat and her father reappeared, and she could tell by the set of his jaw and the restrained violence in his movements that he was incandescent with fury. Most people in the room would not have been able to pick it up. But after thirteen years, Tammy knew the signs.

They both made their way across to her.

"Say goodbye to your Aunt, Tammy," he said. Already, he was magically changing: a weary smile made him seem brave and stoic. "She has to go, unfortunately."

Stunned, Tammy stared at him and then at her aunt. "Now? Already?"

"I'm sorry," her aunt said, holding her eyes. "I was hoping you'd be able to come with me for a little while, but your father doesn't think it's a good idea."

"I want my little girl here," her father said as he smiled at someone over her shoulder and nodded. "We all need to comfort each other, to work together. We must be strong."

Tammy ignored him, aware that he was playing up to any listening ears. "But why do you have to go today, Aunt Nat?"

"I just do." Nat cast a black look at Danny. "I'll be in touch, sweetie. And you can call me any time." She smiled at Tammy. "Want to come and talk while I pack?"

Her father jumped in swiftly. "I think Tammy's place is here, as we celebrate her mother's life. Come and tell us when you're ready to go, so we can farewell you."

Nat looked as though she was going to say something more but then simply nodded. "I'll see you soon, Tammy."

No, you won't, thought Tammy, her gaze immediately going to Garrett on the other side of the room.

She wasn't staying here for even one hour after her aunt had gone.

28

Runaway

TWENTY MINUTES LATER, Tammy stood on the front steps with her father and brothers, watching her Aunt's car disappear around the bend in the driveway. If she stayed there for another few minutes, and kept looking down towards the main road, she would probably be able to catch a glimpse of the car speeding away.

She didn't want to see it.

With her father and brothers there, her Aunt had not been able to say anything more. She had contented herself with a fierce hug and then, holding Tammy's right hand in both of hers, had stared into her eyes. "Be strong, Tammy. I'll call to find out how you're doing soon, all right?" She glanced at Tammy's father. "You have no objection to that, Danny?"

"As long as Tammy's not busy with her homework or other chores, that should be fine," he said shortly.

"Of course," her Aunt said. "If she's tied up when I phone, she can call back as soon as she's free."

Tammy's father had said nothing in reply, and a

sidelong glance at his cool expression told Tammy that messages from her Aunt were unlikely to be passed on.

Now she was gone.

"Well." Tammy's father laid a heavy hand on her shoulder. "That's that, and although I cannot deny that your Aunt had her uses, I have to confess that I will enjoy having peace in our house again. She is, unfortunately, somewhat confrontational." He cleared his throat. "Tomorrow, we'll have a family meeting and decide on household responsibilities and agree on some new rules."

Agree on some new rules, thought Tammy. Like she'd have any say in what the rules were.

"Sure, Dad." Garrett reached over and ruffled Tammy's hair. "Don't worry, Tams; you have two big brothers to watch out for you. Doesn't she, Kyle?"

"Sure does," Kyle said dutifully.

Tammy closed her eyes and forced down the panic rising in her chest. Her fingers clenched around the small folded note that her Aunt had slipped into her hand. "Dad," she said, making her voice sound quiet and submissive, "may I go to my room for a while?"

"Have you thanked everyone who helped us while your mother was sick?"

"Yes, I have," she said quickly. "All the people on the church roster, and everyone who brought food or… or *anything*. Everyone I could think of."

"Hmm." After a moment's silence, her father took his hand from her shoulder. "All right. Marie and Grace have taken charge in the kitchen, and they're leaving covered plates for all of us for supper. Make sure you're in the kitchen at five-thirty."

"Thank you," Tammy said through stiff lips.

It was almost two.

She had three and a half hours to disappear.

"May we be excused too?" Garrett asked. He added quickly, "Kyle and I have thanked everyone already, same as Tams."

For once, his father frowned while looking at him. "It's not appropriate to be off socializing with your friends, Garrett."

"I know that. And really, I don't think I could face them today," Garrett said, his voice sorrowful. "We could just go to Uncle Rocky's, hang out on the verandah. Just talk."

Looking at him, Tammy felt a tired contempt. He was acting again, putting on a face that would impress his father.

"I may need my car."

"We'll go with Uncle Rocky. He'll bring us back at five-thirty," Kyle said, clearly eager to be gone.

"All right." Their father sounded impatient. "All of you, go and do what you want until five-thirty. But when we meet for supper, I want no long faces. We're starting a new phase of our lives. No looking back, no moping, and…" he shot a look at Tammy. "No complaints."

"I'm on board with that," Garrett said, looking his father in the eye. "A new start."

"All right. Go and change out of your good clothes." Her father turned to go back inside, and Tammy whirled and followed on his heels. There was no way she was going to be left alone with her brothers.

She hurried past the still-crowded sitting room, not looking to either side, and rushed into her room. She shut the door behind her, but seconds later, it opened again.

Garrett stuck his head in. "Enjoy your rest," he said. "At five-thirty, everything changes. You heard Dad." He grinned at her and then moved away, leaving the door ajar. Behind him, Kyle laughed, and then their footsteps moved away.

Tammy shut the door again and then finally unfolded the piece of paper that her Aunt had pressed into her hand.

Memorize these phone numbers and call if you need help. The last one is the private detective that I'm using. He'll find me wherever I am. Love you, Tams. Not long now, I promise.

Underneath that, Nat had written three numbers. Hers, her neighbor Molly, and someone called Alec Moore.

Tammy already knew her Aunt's number off by heart. Now she repeated the other two under her breath, over and over, until she could remember every digit.

She kept repeating them while she changed into cut-off denims and a loose shirt, teaming them with sports socks and hardy cross-trainer shoes. Her backpack, hidden outside, contained one full change of clothes, a pair of jeans, and a jacket. She had no idea where she might end up; hitchhiking could well take her to the other side of the country.

Now, for the money. She'd taken a huge risk the night before, slipping into the kitchen late at night and taking the tin out of the top right-hand cupboard. If her father discovered it was missing before the funeral, he'd have raised the roof.

But nobody had realized that the charity box had been raided, and she had carefully folded three hundred dollars into the socks she planned to wear. She had left an IOU in place of the money, so nobody could accuse her of stealing.

Now she was ready.

Although some of their guests had left, she could still hear voices in the kitchen. That didn't matter; she wasn't planning on going that way.

Tammy took one last look around the room she'd slept in for the past thirteen years. All around the dressing-table mirror were tucked photos of her in dress-up clothes from the sessions she'd shared with her mother.

How they'd loved dress-up. And singing.

She walked over and took one of her favorites, where she was dressed as Dorothy from the Wizard of Oz and her mother as the Good Witch.

One day, she'd come back and retrieve all those dress-up clothes from the boxes in the attic. So many memories.

She took a deep breath and edged around the mattress still on the floor from Aunt Nat's visit, then quietly opened the window. A quick peek outside showed her that nobody was in sight, so she slid over the sill and let herself drop into a bed of white pebbles.

A dozen footsteps took her to a row of shrubs bordering the yard, where she bent down low and duck-walked to the cover of more trees and shrubs. As soon as she was out of sight of the house, she ran. Ten minutes later, she was retrieving her backpack from the outskirts of what had been Aunt Nat's target range.

Now that she was committed to the escape, Tammy felt a wild elation. She was getting away. She did *not* have to stay with her father; she would not have to see Garrett ever again.

Whether her Aunt did or didn't find anything to

blackmail her father, she, Tammy Dyson, was never, *never* coming back.

Things didn't go the way Tammy had planned.

She moved carefully through the cover offered by the shrubbery until she reached the road but then grew apprehensive. She squatted down and watched the road for a while through a tracery of leaves, but too many cars were coming from her own house, driven by people she remembered talking with that very afternoon. What if she stepped out on the road to hitchhike and then somebody drove by who recognized her? What if they stopped and called to her? What if they told her father or took note of the license plate of a strange car?

Maybe she should hide somewhere nearby until the next day and *then* hitchhike.

No, by then, the police might be looking for her. Maybe she should wait, go back home and plan her escape on a school day.

No, her mind protested. The image of Garrett loomed large. *No, no, no.*

She couldn't go back.

As though to reinforce her fears, her Uncle Rocky's pickup drove past, taking Garrett and Kyle with him off to his farm.

The farm.

The *Retreat.*

Abruptly, an idea came to her.

People from the Retreat had been at the funeral. Her father had introduced them, Doctor Somebody and Pastor somebody else, and others on the staff.

She could go back and hide in one of the vehicles with the Retreat logo on it and then conceal herself at the farm until it was safer to move on. Nobody would expect her to be out there. She closed her eyes and brought to mind the old outbuildings on the farm. Now that Uncle Rocky was being paid rent for the Retreat, he didn't do any farming, so nobody would go into those old sheds.

She could hide there for a day or two, or even a week, and then make her way to the highway when the fuss had died down. It would be easy to sneak into the kitchen and find food when things were quiet.

It was that or risk being caught hitchhiking.

Decision made, she set off the quarter-mile back to the turnoff to their house, trying to remember the cars that she'd seen outside the house. The Retreat owned a minibus, several SUVs, and a pickup. Only the bus, one of the SUVs, and the pickup had DYSON RETREAT decals on the side.

The pickup would be the best, she decided; the one with a tarp over the tray. She should be able to squeeze in there and hide.

Tammy glanced at her watch. Already, more than an hour of her precious window of time had gone.

She'd better get moving.

29

Investigation

It made Nat's heart ache to leave Tammy behind, but she wasn't going far. Letting Danny think she was on her way back to Chesterfield, she drove instead to a hotel in Baton Rouge and immediately phoned the investigator.

"Hi, Alec. It's Nat," she said without preamble. "Found anything?"

"Hi, Nat." A hesitation. "I thought the funeral was today?"

"It was," she said shortly. "Danny didn't waste any time asking me to leave. I'm staying in Baton Rouge until we wrap this up."

"I see. Just a moment." She heard a rustle of paper, and then he cleared his throat. "There's plenty on Rodney—aka Rocky—Dyson, but you already knew that. From what I can find out, he seems to have turned over a new leaf. He still has outstanding traffic violations, but nothing else for the past three years."

She made the connection instantly. "Since the Retreat opened."

"More or less. But he's earning well over and above

what you say Danny's records indicated." He paused. "Looks like there might be some substance to what Chase Gilmore told you."

Her pulse quickened. "What have you found?"

"No evidence so far, but I have the place under surveillance. I'm doing this in shifts with one of my contractors. Nat, this could get expensive if it goes on for weeks. Chase saw only three lots processed during his time there, you say? It may even be months."

Nat pictured her bank account. While it wasn't anywhere near as swollen as Danny Dyson's, it was healthy enough. She'd had nothing much to spend her earnings on for many years. "As long as we get results. Let me know as soon as you can, Alec. I've got to get Tammy out of there."

"I'll be doing surveillance again tonight."

"I'll call you tomorrow. Say, nine a.m.?"

"That'll be fine."

Nat hung up and looked around her at her motel suite. Home, for however long it took.

It was time she contacted the Rifle Club back home and let them know that she might be away for another month yet. But to cover her trail, she'd let them think she was on her way home—just in case Danny called to check up on her.

She unzipped her suitcase and pulled out the files she'd copied. Now that she was out of the house, she'd go over them again, with no worries about being interrupted. She could well have missed something, the way she'd always been looking over her shoulder in case Danny found her with copies of his files.

Danny Dyson was furious. It was five-forty-five, fifteen minutes after the time he had decreed his family should all meet in the kitchen, and Tammy was nowhere to be found.

Garrett and Kyle had dutifully returned half an hour earlier, but neither had any idea where their sister might be.

Danny closed his eyes and breathed in slowly. *One, two, three…* He tamped down on the rage that threatened to engulf him.

On the very day of Susannah's funeral, his daughter had chosen to flout his orders. That showed no respect at all for her mother's memory—no respect for *him.*

He spoke slowly and calmly, looking from Garrett to Kyle. "So, neither of you have seen her since your Aunt Natalie left."

They both shook their heads.

"What time did you go to your Uncle's place?"

Garrett glanced at Kyle. "Uh…two-thirty, was it? About then, I think."

Danny tapped his fingers on the table and went over his own movements. He'd smiled and patted backs and submitted to hugs from church people until he thought he might go mad and then thanked the ladies from the church at least six times, individually and collectively. Then he'd finally waved goodbye to the last of them and retreated to his home office with Terrence Busby.

Busby was the only man who knew enough to hurt him.

But then, if Terrence ever said anything, he'd be torpedoing his own career as well. His whole *life.* He had as much to lose as Danny.

After Terrence had offered his condolences, they'd

spent fifteen minutes in small talk and then touched on future plans. Which, although they could no longer include Susannah, looked like they might free him from the tyranny of pretending that he cared about his so-called parishioners. Well, not *his* parishioners, exactly, but close enough as far as they were concerned. Most of them came to Danny in preference to the pastor anyway.

When Terrence left, Danny was at last alone with his thoughts. He allowed himself a few brief moments of grief and anger at the injustice of having Susannah taken from him, and then his thoughts turned to his children.

Garrett, he was proud of; a promising young man who was already following in his father's footsteps. Smart and charming, he would be a huge business asset. Danny saw a lot of himself in Garrett, and soon, he would start to educate the boy about how the world really worked. He had a feeling that his son wouldn't be too surprised to hear that his father was a rich man, destined to grow a lot richer.

Garrett could spend his time at college making useful contacts.

And then there was Kyle, not too bright but malleable, like his uncle. Rocky had been well pleased with Kyle over the past few months. There was a lot that Danny would *not* be sharing with Kyle, but he could teach Garrett how to use his brother. Kyle was a good son, albeit one who might take the wrong path if he didn't receive strong guidance.

Finally, Tammy. With a spike of resentment and dislike, he thought about his thirteen-year-old daughter, so like her mother in looks, yet miles away in temperament. Susannah had been all sweetness and light and forgiveness. Talented, beautiful... what Tammy *could* have been if she hadn't been born with that rebellious streak.

She had taken far too much of Susannah's attention away from him, but she, too, could be molded into something useful. Tammy was young yet. He had years to bend her character the way he wanted it, and eventually, he would steer her into a marriage that would benefit him.

Tammy, he had already admitted to himself, would need a strong husband. One who would ensure her obedience, making sure that she would present just the image he wanted to the outside world. Properly trained, she could use her looks to advantage.

"Dad?"

The sound of Garrett's voice brought Danny's attention back to the present, and he could tell from the expression on the boys' faces that he'd been sitting there tied up in his thoughts for some time.

"What do you want us to do?" Garrett ventured. "Go out and look for her?"

Danny looked at him. "Where?"

"She's probably hiding out somewhere nearby and sulking," Garrett said. "She sits on that old bench seat up near the back fence sometimes."

Another glance at the clock showed him that Tammy was now twenty minutes late. "All right. See if you can find her, and if you do, don't put up with any tears or tantrums. Just bring her to me, whether she wants to come or not. Your sister needs to learn her place in this household immediately."

"Right." Garrett jumped up, and although his face

was serious, Danny could tell that he was quite prepared to drag his sister back home.

And who could blame him? After the years of lies she'd been spreading about her brother, maybe it was time he got some of his own back.

"Be back here in no later than half an hour," Danny ordered.

His sons hurried off, and Danny poured himself a whiskey.

This was all he needed for supper, he thought darkly, and then sat to wait for his sons to bring back his infuriating daughter.

Fifteen miles away, Tammy imagined his reaction when she had failed to show. His eyes would be like black stones, devoid of the twinkle that he could conjure up on will for the church family. His lips would be pressed tight, and he'd be snarling at her brothers, demanding to know why she wasn't there.

The very thought of his humorless face brought back the familiar cold, tight feeling in her chest.

They'd be out looking for her.

Panic made her breath catch in her throat, but she pushed it away and dug into her backpack for an apple. Later—much, much later when everyone was asleep— she would sneak into Uncle Rocky's kitchen and find something else. It was still light outside, which was good because she could see her surroundings.

She had avoided a couple of newish-looking sheds and hurried to the smallest of the old ones, some distance from the main house. She had no idea what it had originally been used for, but she remembered being in it a couple of times when her parents visited, and she and her brothers had been ordered outside to play with their older cousin. The three boys had converted it into a kind of clubhouse and laughed at her tears when she failed initiations to in their secret club. She had vague memories of being made to carry heavy stones and to stand with her hands above her head for a long, long time.

She never was admitted to the club, but they let her play prisoner.

The shed smelled of damp earth and mold, and the filthy, threadbare sofa in one corner was barely visible under boxes and rusty tools.

Tammy shuddered and flattened an empty cardboard box. That would do to sit on for a while. When she went to the house, she could grab a sheet or blanket out of the linen closet and make up a bed on the sofa.

It was only for a few days.

Her leg throbbed, and Tammy inspected it again, gingerly touching the torn flesh. The tray of the pickup had been filled with gardening tools, and every time the Retreat's gardener had driven over a rough section of road or hurtled around a corner, Tammy had been flung against something with hard edges.

When the truck had finally stopped, and the driver's door opened and closed, Tammy had stared at the tarpaulin above her head, quaking. Would he notice that the edge of the tarpaulin wasn't tied down? Or flip it open to take something out of the back?

He didn't. She heard footsteps receding into the distance and had waited a long, long time, ears pricked, to ensure that nobody was there when she peeked out.

The pickup was parked under a long carport with two other work vehicles and a ride-on lawnmower. In the distance, beyond a neat hedge, she could see an extensive low building that looked like a motel.

The Retreat. She had been there a couple of times, once when it opened and once when they'd had a Christmas party with the staff.

Ready to bolt if anyone saw her, Tammy climbed out, hauled her backpack after her, and started to make her way cautiously to the old farm visible some distance away. She took her time, using anything that offered cover and sprinting across open areas.

Not a single soul saw her.

30

Missing

WITHIN 48 HOURS, the news of 13-year-old Tammy Dyson's disappearance had swept through Baton Rouge. Danny Dyson, the grieving widower, cut a tragic figure on television as he expressed his fears for his daughter's safety and implored her to come home. Her brother Garrett, tragically similar in looks to his recently deceased mother and missing sister, added his heartfelt plea for her to return to them.

So sad, the community all agreed. Clearly, the little girl was devastated at the loss of her mother and was not thinking clearly. The church provided some video clips of Tammy and her mother singing a duet at church, looking like blond angels. Reports of sightings began to trickle in, but none led to Tammy's return.

Local law enforcement guardedly agreed there was a concern that the girl might have been picked up by a predator, but given the circumstances, they were still treating her as a runaway.

Nat heard the news from her private investigator. He phoned at midday the next day, just three hours after his first report of the day about his surveillance of the Dyson farm.

"Have you heard about Tammy, Nat?" he said the moment she snatched up the phone at the motel.

Nat's heart clenched. "No. What?"

"It seems she's run away."

For a moment, Nat couldn't speak. *Oh, Tammy. Why couldn't you hold on, just for a few days?*

"The last time anyone saw her was just after you left," he said. "I talked to a contact at the station. They're trying to track you down, Nat; Danny has apparently suggested that Tammy might be with you."

Fury leaped within her, and she spat out a few uncomplimentary words. "He would. Well, he needn't worry; I'll soon lay that fear to rest."

"There was a brief mention on the radio this morning, so you can tell them that's where you heard it. Not from me…that would lead to questions, and we don't want Danny to catch wind of what we're doing."

"Right." Overcome with fear for Tammy; Nat leaned her forehead against the wall. "Where would she go? What should I do now?"

"There's probably not a lot you *can* do unless you know where she might have gone. The police are on the lookout. "

Nat tried to organize her thoughts. "I gave her three phone numbers. Mine, a neighbor of mine back in Chesterfield, and yours. I told her to phone any of them if she needed help."

"I'll let you know right away if she contacts me. I'm sorry, Nat."

"Okay. I need to think… Alec, can you hire someone else? To watch Garrett? Danny wouldn't harm her physically, I'm sure, but that brother of hers… I don't trust him."

"You don't think he's behind her disappearance?"

"I don't think so. But who knows? He's dangerous, Alec. Verging on psychopathic, even. So can you? Find someone?"

"I can, yes. But you're already paying for Stuart and me to do surveillance on the Retreat, and now if you want me to put someone else on, it's—"

"It's going to cost, I know. I don't care. We've got to find her."

"All right. Call me back in an hour, and I'll tell you what I've been able to arrange."

Two Days Later

On the third night after her escape, Tammy waited until after midnight to set off on her nightly forage. Her uncle lived alone, now that his son had moved away, and seemed to be a heavy sleeper. It had been ridiculously easy, skulking through the shadows to the dark veranda of the farmhouse and letting herself in through the unlocked wet area near the kitchen. Uncle Rocky seemed to favor a diet of meat, potatoes, and assorted junk food, but all she cared about was finding enough to stop her from going hungry. From the boxes in the trash, she could see that much of the food came from the Retreat's kitchens.

She quietly filled a plastic shopping bag with a packet of chips, bread, a few cans of soft drink, and some sliced ham, then made her way to the door. She had just stepped outside, carefully pulling the door closed behind her, when a light went on inside, throwing a rectangle of light onto the verandah.

It was from her uncle's bedroom.

Her heart giving a gigantic leap, Tammy threw herself down the steps and dived behind an overgrown shrub, squirming in as far as possible, hugging the plastic bag to her. She'd made too much noise. Any moment, he would be coming out looking for intruders….

Then she heard the muted sound of an engine, and as her uncle came out of the house and walked down the steps, just inches from her hiding place, the dark bulk of a truck trundled through the gate and continued along the road that ran past the house.

Tammy pushed through spiky branches to the side of the house and peered around the corner of the farmhouse, watching. He *hadn't* heard her! He had been waiting for this truck.

Which meant that he hadn't been sleeping, and if she hadn't been so quiet, he would have caught her. For a moment, she was light-headed at the thought.

Her uncle walked behind the truck until it stopped outside one of the new sheds. The driver's door opened and closed softly, and she could see the vague outline of a man getting out. She could hear men talking softly but couldn't make out the actual words. The brake lights of the truck flared once and went dark.

Tammy had heard rumors about her Uncle and had caught one or two conversations between her mother and father. She knew that her uncle had been in trouble with the law but was now supposed to be turning over a new leaf.

Trying to make sense of the activity here in the middle of the night, she wasn't so sure about that.

There was a dull squeal of hinges as the back doors of the truck were opened. More dark shapes climbed out.

Lots of activity…lots of *people.*

The group all moved around the truck into the now-open shed, and then the door to *that* closed. Nobody turned on the lights until the door was closed; then, all she could see was a faint glow underneath the door.

Someone climbed back into the driver's seat of the truck, and it backed up, turned around, and slowly drove back past her and out onto the road.

Tammy's breath finally slowed. She had gone so close to being caught. So *close.*

Shivering more from adrenalin than cold, she pulled her knees up to her chin and stayed where she was, not daring to move. A seemingly interminable time later, she heard footsteps approaching, and then her uncle's heavy tread went past her again, up the steps and inside.

Five minutes after that, the light went out.

Tammy waited until it had been quiet a long time, and then, her heart in her mouth, hurried back to her refuge.

She didn't care what her Uncle Rocky was up to. She just wanted to be *out* of here.

Secreted in the same spot he'd been hiding for the past week, Alec scribbled down the registration plate of the truck. He had debated whether to follow it, but right now, he was more interested in its cargo. Better to hang around and see what else he could find out.

It seemed the information that Nat had bought from

Chase Gilmore had been good. Now he just needed to get closer so he could get some decent photos, the evidence that Nat needed.

But it wasn't only the cargo onboard the truck that had his pulse racing. It was the unexpected sight of a missing thirteen-year-old girl, briefly illuminated by the light thrown from a window, throwing herself down the steps of the farmhouse. He hadn't seen her go in, and if Rocky Dyson hadn't turned on a light at the crucial moment, he might not have seen her at all.

He watched the whole scene play out until the girl finally emerged from the bushes, just a dark shadow in the night. He watched her make her way up the hill until she slipped inside the wreck of a shed up near the back fence.

So *that* was where she was hiding. At least she was safe, not alone and on the run, at the mercy of any lowlife on the road. He debated with himself for a few moments and then made a decision.

He couldn't risk her being found, and he couldn't risk her disappearing again.

Alec quietly made his way to the shed, circled it once to check that there were no easy exits, and then tapped on the door while he called her name softly. "Tammy?"

No answer. Of course not; she wouldn't give herself up that easily.

"Tammy," he said in a low voice, worried about sound carrying at night. "It's Alec here. Alec Moore—I'm a private investigator. Your Aunt Nat told me she gave you my phone number, that you could trust me."

Silence.

He didn't want to terrify her more than she was already.

"Tammy? I saw you while I was doing surveillance. Please.… Your aunt is worried out of her mind. She needs to know you're okay."

Silence.

Then a voice suddenly said, from the other side of the door, "How do I know you're really Alec Moore?"

"Sssh. Keep it down. Do you remember the number Nat gave you?"

"Yes."

"Okay. Here it is." He recited his number for her.

Silence again, and then: "I still don't know that it's you."

He sighed and decided that honesty was the only thing that would work with this child. "Who else would be keeping watch here at night, trying to find out what's going on? I know Nat told you that she was looking for something to force your father to give you up."

After a few moments, the door creaked open towards him, just a crack. "That truck tonight," she whispered. "Is that part of it?"

"Yes," he said, "I think so."

"Is it against the law?"

"If it's what we think it is."

The door opened further to reveal Tammy standing there. She crossed her arms tightly in front of her. "*What* do you think it is?"

He shook his head. The kid wasn't going to give in easily. "Probably people trafficking. Illegals."

"Where is Aunt Nat?"

"In Baton Rouge, in a motel. She's been there ever since she left your house."

"She didn't go back home to Chesterfield?"

"She refused to go home and leave you here. She

hired someone else to look for you, too—but of course, we didn't know you were so close."

In the moonlight, he could see her lips part in a fleeting smile.

"If you take me to Aunt Nat, will I have to go back to Dad?"

He smiled grimly, thinking of the information he and Nat already had and what tomorrow's photo opportunities might bring. "I think we might have enough now to keep you safe."

Tammy stared at him. "What if someone's watching Aunt Nat's motel like you're watching here?"

He had to stifle a chuckle. "You know what?" he whispered. "You're thinking like an investigator. All right, what if I take you to my office and ask Nat to meet us there?"

"Okay," she said abruptly and disappeared, then came back with a backpack. "Let's go."

Torn, he glanced over his shoulder at the new sheds, down near the house. "Tammy, we can't go right now. You saw those people going into the shed?"

She nodded.

"I can't risk their being removed while I'm not here. I have to stick around until my relief arrives, try to get photos."

She sighed, a tiny sigh that he barely heard, but he felt it spear through his heart. The shed smelled of dirt and decay and mold, and she'd been here for three days.

Alec made a decision. "You can wait in my car if you like. I always keep a blanket and pillow in the back seat for surveillance. It's probably more comfortable than here, so you might catch a couple of hours. I'm sorry, I know you'd like to see your aunt right away."

"That's okay," she said stoically. "Where's the car?"

"Just off the road, behind some trees. Nobody can see it from the road. I'll take you there and then come back and keep watching. Okay?"

She made a small noise of assent.

Like thieves in the night, they both slipped through the shadows and across the fields to where his car was hidden. When she was tucked up with a blanket on the back seat, he left her there with the doors locked and instructions to hide if she heard anyone approach.

Not the best solution, but better than what lay ahead of her with Danny Dyson.

Armed with his camera and a flashlight, he continued surveillance until dawn.

It was worth it.

31

Ultimatum

Two days later

IT WAS midday when Nat drew up outside Danny Dyson's home, parking between Danny's car and a champagne-colored BMW with a registration plate that began with TB. Terrence Busby's vehicle.

She sat for a moment, rehearsing what she planned to say. She was aware—as was Alec—that hiding Tammy when the police were looking for her was likely to land her in hot water if it came to light, but the stakes in this game were high.

Just in case she needed it, Nat clicked the 'record' button on her new voice recorder, slipped it into her pocket, and picked up the bulky envelope on the seat beside her.

She had to knock three times before Danny opened the door, but that didn't surprise her. Keeping her waiting would be part of his game.

His face gave nothing away when his eyes met hers. *Danny Poker Face.*

"Hello, Natalie," he said, his voice level. His gaze moved over her shoulder to her car. "I see Tammy isn't with you."

"I've already told you that I'm not behind your daughter's disappearance," she said. "But you'll want to hear what I have to say. Can we not waste time?"

"Terrence Busby has had to postpone a meeting with an important client to be here," he said. "You have ten minutes, and then he has to leave." He still didn't step back to let her inside.

"Fine," she said. "I doubt he'll want to rush off once he sees what I bring with me, but that's up to him."

A tiny muscle jumped in his jaw, and he waved her inside.

As she had expected, he had chosen his office for the meeting. Terrence was already seated in one of the easy chairs around the coffee table. Danny took the other, waving her to the two-seater sofa.

Terrence looked at her with disapproval. "If you're here to ask for custody of your niece, I can tell you now that you're wasting your time. Danny is a valuable member of the community, held in high esteem, with an enormous amount of support from his church. Tammy couldn't be in better hands."

Natalie smiled. "You really think so?"

Danny heaved a martyred sigh. "Terrence is well aware of your attitude, and we know that you've been talking to Loretta Paxton and Therese Gilmore...and others. I have contacts everywhere, Natalie. If you have some idea in your head about stirring up trouble, accusing me of undue influence to obtain financial gain, it won't hold water. There are out-of-court settlements in play here."

"Yes, I know," Nat said. "Danny-the-Saint-Dyson is known to have plowed back bequests into the church, yadda yadda yadda."

Terrence Busby pointedly looked at his watch. "Unless you have something of value to say, I'm wasting my time being here. Let's cut to the chase. Are you hiding Tammy Dyson?"

Nat raised an eyebrow. "Feel free to leave, then, Terrence. I'll just have a quiet chat to Danny about his secret bank accounts in a different city, including deposits that came from you."

His eyes narrowed. Beside him, Danny shifted in his seat and sat up a little straighter.

"I have no idea what you mean."

"Oh, I think you do." Nat opened the envelope on her lap, conscious of the two men watching her. She plucked out several sheets on the top of the sheaf of papers and photos inside. "As of a few weeks ago, Danny, your bank balance was close enough to one point three million. That's in just one bank account. I'm sure if the right people went digging, they'd find more." She leaned forward and offered him the papers. "I'm quite prepared to seek out the right people."

Expressionless, he took them from her, ran his gaze down the columns of figures, and then passed them across to Terrence.

"Your official bank account, of course, isn't anywhere near that," she said. "About sixty grand in savings, I believe? Plus, a regular income from your work at the Retreat. A humble income, after very generous deductions for the church."

He folded his arms and waited for her to go on.

Nat looked at Terrence. "Do you still want to hurry off to your next appointment?"

Not as good as Danny at hiding his feelings, he glared at her. "Say what you have to say."

She debated her next move. The photos of the boys bullying Tammy, she thought. She'd save the ones at Rocky's farm for last.

Slowly, she dipped into the envelope and drew out the photos, then sat forward to fan them out on the coffee table. "These are photos I took of Garrett and Kyle with Tammy after school. They've been making her life a complete misery. Look at the expression on her face, Danny." Despite her resolve to stay calm, her voice grew heated. "Garrett calls this 'having a bit of fun'. Does Tammy look like she's enjoying it? Or does she look like she's being held against her will?"

Danny stared at the photos. "I didn't know this was going on."

"Tammy tells me she's tried to tell you, many times, about how Garrett hurts her and sets her up. You always believe him, not her."

He breathed in and out slowly, several times, and then raised his eyes, cold as ice, to hers. "I'll speak with them. It won't happen again."

"Unless you're with her twenty-four hours a day, it *will* happen again, believe me. Your precious Garrett is cruel and vindictive, and Kyle is almost as bad."

There was another brief silence, and then Terrence spoke up. "What exactly do you want?"

"You already know, Terrence. I want custody of Tammy. Full custody until she's of age."

"That's not going to happen," Danny said coldly. "You've got details of a bank account and a few photos.

I have the support of a whole community and a lot of influence."

"I thought you might say that." Nat looked at him scornfully. "I didn't expect you to give in easily; you're too full of your own importance. But I'm sure that giving up Tammy is preferable to a prison sentence."

"Now you're being ridiculous. Nothing I've done could possibly see me land in prison." Danny shot a look at Terrence. "I've paid all my taxes."

"I'm not talking about the IRS." Nat decided it was time to play her ace. "I'm talking about *this.*"

She pulled another sheaf of photos from the envelope and slapped them down in front of the two men, one at a time. "Rocky's farm. Special deliveries at night. Deliveries that involve not goods, but *people*…oh, and what do we have here? Yes, that's *Kyle* you can see there, Danny, with his uncle. Talking to certain people that have no business being anywhere near your high-end *Retreat.*"

Finally, Danny's composure cracked. "Where did you get these?"

"I have plenty of money. I was willing to pay the right people to get my niece out of your hands." Nat extracted the last sheet of paper from the envelope and tossed it down on the photos. "Names and addresses. And all I have to do is say the word, and this information will be released. Naturally, these are all just copies."

She sat back, drinking in the fury and fear on the faces of the two men. "Your traffic in illegal immigrants stops right here and now, Danny. And you can use part of that million-plus you have salted away to give money back to the rightful heirs that have seen their inheritance go to you. From now on, you will *not* encourage anyone else to leave money to you or the church. Apart from that…well, as long as Tammy remains in my care, none of this goes to the proper authorities."

"That makes you an accessory, you realize," Terrence said spitefully.

"Perhaps it does," Nat said, looking at him coldly. "But luckily for you, Tammy is more important than anything else right now."

"We have no guarantee that you'll sit on this either," Danny said.

"I have no desire to put Tammy through any more than she's had to suffer already. I just want to leave here, with her, and never set eyes on you again."

The two men looked at each other, Danny's jaw working as he got his emotions under control. Finally, he spat out, "Do it, Terrence. Draw it up."

"Thank you," said Natalie. "I'll come to your office within the hour, Terrence, to pick up the papers. They'll show Danny has agreed that his niece needs a woman's care in her formative teenage years. Just make sure that there are no loopholes that allow Danny to take her back because I'll be getting top legal advice."

She stood up and shouldered her bag, waving at the papers and photos spilled over the coffee table. "Keep all this. I have copies, hidden safely."

Danny stood up too, his eyes holding hers. The black, cold depths chilled her to the bone.

"Where is she?"

"In about an hour, after I have a signed custody agreement and tell her it's safe, she'll turn herself in at the police station," Nat said. "She will ask for me. *Only* me. So don't try to see her, Danny."

Without another glance, she left.

A Promise

Letting the curtain drop back into place after checking that Natalie Arnold was indeed driving away, Danny turned to Terrence.

"Find out who's been feeding her all this. We need to ensure that anyone who knows anything is silenced."

"I can't do that in the next half hour." Terrence glared at him. "And some of it, she could have found right here in this house. Did she have access to your office?"

"I didn't lock the door, but the filing cabinet was always locked. *Always.*"

"Where do you keep the key?"

Danny plucked the ring of keys out of his pocket and shook them in Terrence's face, annoyed at the implication. "Right here with me. All the time. There's no way she could have gotten hold of it."

Terrence frowned. "What about at night? When you sleep?"

"I keep them with me. And I slept lightly because of

Susannah the whole time she was here. There's no way she could get them."

His attorney looked unconvinced. "What about a spare key?"

"There isn't one."

Terrence made a short, angry, dismissive movement with his hand. "All right. The fact remains, she got hold of the information somehow. And how did she find out about what's going on at Rocky's? When did she go out there?"

"I'd know if she'd been out there. It's come from somewhere else."

The other man's eyes narrowed. "Kyle?"

Danny let out a derisive laugh. "He can't stand her. No way she'd get it from him."

"Then someone else. Someone who worked there or at the Retreat. *Someone* figured out what was going on… and told her."

Danny turned away, his mind racing. Who? *Who?*

She'd been talking to Loretta; his sources knew that much. And Tina May and David Caraway, the other disgruntled heirs who had taken action. That's how she'd know about the bequests that came his way. She'd clearly lain in wait for Garrett—*stupid* Garrett!—after school after becoming suspicious. But the illegal immigrant trail…*how?*

He'd figure it out. And whoever had spoken out of turn would pay for it.

He slapped his hand against the wall. "We can work it out later. For now, go and write up some agreement awarding custody of the girl to Natalie. Make it sound as though I'm making a sacrifice for a vulnerable young teenager. And if you can, leave in a loophole."

"That would be easy if this were a straightforward case," Terrence snapped. "But with a prison sentence hanging over both our heads and her threat to run any custody arrangement by a top legal counsel? Forget loopholes. You've never had any time for the girl anyway."

Danny went still.

Deep breathing. One…two…three.

He turned to Terrence and said in a voice deliberately low and silky with menace, "Don't you ever say that to me again and especially don't ever repeat it to anyone else. As far as the rest of the world is concerned, my daughter is everything to me. *Everything.* It breaks my heart to part with her. Understand?"

Terrence rolled his eyes. "Whatever you say."

"Go. I'm going to see Rocky."

He stood on the top step and watched Terrence drive away, thinking about what it all meant.

The lucrative trade in human trafficking, shut down, just like that. The door to future bequests from susceptible parishioners—*closed.* Not to mention a good chunk of his savings gone to guarantee Natalie Arnold's continued silence.

And no more Susannah.

Pure, black hatred for his sister-in-law and his traitorous daughter consumed him. He'd do whatever needed to be done to protect himself now, but he'd find out who had been talking.

They would pay for this.

He could start again, he promised himself, and even if it took him the rest of his life, both Natalie and Tammy would rue the day they took on Danny Dyson.

33

Que Sera Sera

TAMMY SAT in her aunt's car, watching the road unwind before them. She was still tense, even though Aunt Nat had shown her the legal document to say that she had custody.

She didn't trust her father.

She wouldn't, in fact, be one bit surprised if he somehow stopped them before they left the state and made her go back with him.

"I don't think the police believed me," she said quietly.

"Yes, they did," her aunt said. "Alec used to work on the police force there; they still talk to him. And most of what you said was the truth. You stowed away in the Retreat pickup and hid out in the old shed at your uncle's. You just didn't tell them about the truck in the middle of the night."

"They kept asking me questions about the lady in the white van. They said they hadn't been able to find her."

"They probably didn't hold out much hope. That's

why we told you to say you caught a lift in a white van. There are a million of them out there."

Tammy was silent. "What if he changes his mind and comes to get me?"

"He won't, unless he is prepared to go to prison."

"What if Garrett comes to find me?"

Her aunt grinned and patted Tammy on the knee. "Not going to happen, but if he does? I can outshoot Garrett."

Tammy wasn't reassured. "Would you really shoot him?"

"No. But just because we've left town, Tammy, it doesn't mean that I've stopped. Alec is going to keep digging and finding out whatever he can about your father and your two brothers. We've got Danny tied up, and Kyle's in it up to his neck, but Garrett...." her aunt's voice suddenly sounded tired. "I can't believe you're the only one that Garrett has treated in that way. I believe something else will come to light...if not now, then soon. If he ever turns up at the door, I'll be ready."

Tammy wasn't reassured. Garrett was smooth-tongued, sure, but he was sneaky enough to just grab what he wanted and run without being seen.

Her aunt seemed to guess what was going through her mind. "He won't come after you now, Tammy. Your father will see to that. Garrett has a football career ahead of him, and college. He'll have more than you to worry about. You were just a convenient target."

When Tammy said nothing, her aunt sighed. "What worries you most?"

"Garrett. *Everything* about Garrett," Tammy said immediately. "The look on his face that time...I thought he really wanted to kill me." She thought of the photos that her aunt had shown her, telling her that Garrett wouldn't want the church people to see them—wouldn't want *anyone* to see them. In one photo, Aunt Nat had captured his face twisted, leering, *evil*…

Her aunt was silent for a long while, but when she did speak, her voice was decisive.

"Here's what we're going to do, Tammy. I know you've never held a gun, but I'm going to teach you to shoot. Better than that, I'm going to teach you to be an *expert* shot, through the competition circuit. I hope that you'll never need to use a gun against another human being —Garrett or anyone else—but it will give you confidence. You'll learn a lot through the discipline."

Tammy felt a spark of interest. "You will?"

"Would you like that?"

"Yes. *Yes*, please."

"Then it's done."

They drove for another fifteen minutes without speaking while Tammy thought about her new life. "When I live with you, will I go to church?"

"Would you like to?"

"Yes. I think so. I liked Grace and Marie and the choir. Can I sing there?"

"I have no idea, but we'll find out."

Out of the corner of her eye, Tammy saw her aunt looking at her. "Do you dance, Tammy?"

"No. Well, Mom and I used to…" for a second she choked, but forced herself to continue, "We used to dance around and pretend, like the people in old movies, but I don't know how to dance properly."

"Then I'll introduce you to Miss Molly. She lives near me, and she lives and breathes dancing. She used to be a ballroom dancing gold medalist and has all these beautiful dresses. She's a *wonderful* dancer."

Tammy thought about dancing and singing and dressing up, and her heart eased slightly.

"Miss Molly goes to vintage trailer meets," her aunt went on, her voice becoming enthusiastic. "They all dress up in rock'n'roll clothes and sing old hits and stay in these cute little old trailers. It's not just older people. That might be fun."

"Ye-es," Tammy said cautiously. She liked the sound of the rock'n'roll, but old trailers? And old people? "Maybe."

"You've got plenty of time to decide. I want you to have fun, Tammy. Do all the things that teenage girls love to do." Her aunt laughed. "Except you'll have a little bit of Annie Oakley in you. A crack shot."

Tammy glanced at the side mirror and then twisted around to see the road behind.

Nobody was coming after them.

She really was going to start a new life.

With a huge sigh, Tammy leaned her head on the side window and closed her eyes.

"A new start," her aunt said. "Remember what your Mom said. The future's not ours to see…but we sure can shape it to be the way we want."

Yes, thought Tammy drowsily.

Que Sera Sera.

What will be, will be.

FROM THE AUTHOR

The story you've just finished reading gives you a few hints about Tammy's early life, and the people who had the most influence on her in her teenage years: her aunt Nat and Miss Molly, the delightful dance instructor who encouraged Tammy to follow her love of song and dance—and of course, introduced her to the world of retro trailers! I've had a number of people curious to know more about Tammy (after a hint here and there in earlier books), so now you know…*some* of it, anyway!

And I have an invitation for you! Would you like to join my readers' group?

Subscribe to my newsletter, and you'll be sure to hear about new releases, bargain books, and other great reads! I have a special welcome gift for members, too: a prequel to the Georgie series called *Fortune's Wheel.*

A lot of my readers are enjoying this little book: It's Rosa's story, tracing her life with gypsies and her overwhelming love for Georgie from the moment she was born. I think you'll love it! Join us here:

https://www.margmcalister.com/free-georgie-book/

Until next time...
Marg

ABOUT THE AUTHOR

Marg McAlister is the author of the popular Georgie B. Goode Cozy Mystery series (set in the USA) and Series 2 (Australian RV Adventure series), also featuring Georgie.

Marg lives by the sea on the mid-north coast of NSW, but she and her husband spend part of the year on The Gemfields in Central Queensland, living off the grid on their mining claim. While her husband digs for sapphires and zircons, operates the wash plant and drives around dirt tracks, Marg is usually writing—or socializing!

Marg is also the author of a series of books for aspiring writers, and the owner of Blue Gem Publishing, which publishes books in a range of genres.

www.ingramcontent.com/pod-product-compliance
Lightning Source LLC
Chambersburg PA
CBHW020813190726
48285CB00006B/2268